A Taste to Die For

A Taste to Die For

Culinary Crimes

Culinary Crimes

BOB SCHUCK

YELLOWBACK MYSTERIES
JAMES A. ROCK & COMPANY, PUBLISHERS
FLORENCE • SOUTH CAROLINA

Address comments and inquiries to:

YELLOWBACK MYSTERIES
James A. Rock & Company, Publishers
1937 West Palmetto Street, #6
Florence, SC 29501

E-mail:
jrock@rockpublishing.com   lrock@rockpublishing.com
Internet URL: www.rockpublishing.com

Paperback ISBN: 978-1-59663-807-5

Library of Congress Control Number: 2009926705

Printed in the United States of America

First Edition: 2015

This lovely little tome

is dedicated to

my wonderful wife

Margaret

and

my children

Robbie and Hannah

with thanks for

their love and

support

ACKNOWLEDGEMENTS

Many thanks to all the important persons who helped me along the way and whose patience and assistance were most greatly appreciated. Thanks, especially, to my parents who always set the example of honesty and hard work; to my brothers Tom, Bill, and Jim who have always tried to be there for me; to my cousins, Lee and Jacintha, for their love and encouragement; to Alberta who helped me get started; to my editors, Alan Abrams and Jan Wagner, for their help and inspiration; and to the good Lord, who has helped me, sometimes in spite of myself.

THE RECIPE FOR WALDO PRIDE'S DELUXE FRUITCAKE

We regret to inform you that, just prior to going to press, Mr. Pride informed the publisher that he no longer wished to share his secret recipe. He advises that his fruitcake is now being marketed as "A Taste To Die For" and may be found at fine stores everywhere, and perhaps on cable shopping channels and the web.

PROLOGUE

Partially clothed in shadow, a lone figure wearing yellow rubber gloves sits staring at the blank TV screen. With the click of a button, the VCR begins to play a scene from the black and white version of *Arsenic and Old Lace*.

The machine itself practically knows where to cue the tape to the desired scene because it has been watched so many times before. The viewer leans in, anticipating, breathlessly studying the action and the dialogue.

The two old maids are telling their horrified nephew how they dispose of elderly gentlemen by poisoning them with their homemade Elderberry wine.

The scene ends. The viewer stops the tape, sits back in the chair, and chuckles.

CHAPTER 1

The male nurse had just finished helping Margaret Majors back to her hospital bed from the bathroom. It was such an effort for her to walk because of the pain in her left hip. Exhausted, she thanked him as he lifted her legs into bed.

Suddenly, there was a sensation in her chest unlike anything she had ever felt before. It took her breath away, literally—and then my mother was gone.

I like to think that my grandmother was waiting on the other side to welcome and reassure her, as my mother looked back over her shoulder with concern for me and my two older brothers, for whom she had sacrificed everything.

The night before my mother died, I had stumbled into the Hollywood apartment I shared with two other guys, dropped my bags by the door and fell into bed, exhausted and bleary-eyed after what seemed like forever trying to get a flight out of Detroit in the middle of a blizzard. It was December 27, 1988, and my father had put me on a plane back to Los Angeles via San Francisco, which was the only flight available. I was returning from what I thought would probably be my last Christmas visit to Ohio for a long, long time ... little did I know.

I had always looked forward to going home to Ohio for the holidays, but now things seemed different. During a Christmas party at a friend's house in L.A., I felt like I had finally found where I belonged. It was one of those magical moments when time stands still. The weather was perfect. I had wonderful friends. And most of all, I was doing what I wanted—pursuing my dream of becoming a writer for network television. Or, perhaps more to the point, communicating a positive message to a nation I believed was hungry for one.

I also had another purpose in going home that Christmas. My mother had developed an as yet undiagnosed problem with her left hip sometime in September. The pain had become so bad she had been reduced to walking with a cane. The doctors tried everything short of surgery to determine the problem, but as yet without success. No one dared mention the "C" word. That was unthinkable.

It was unthinkable that this woman who had left home in 1932 at the age of 15 to attend college and who subsequently attended law school and was admitted to the Ohio State Bar in 1939 while still three months shy of her 22nd birthday, could succumb to cancer. Unthinkable that this woman who had served as Probate and Juvenile Judge in the early 1960's—at a time when women didn't do such things—could be terminally ill. Unthinkable that this woman, who had been defeated for reelection after our father had left her and then started a law practice from scratch at the age of 50 so she could raise and educate three sons, could be beaten by anything. Margaret Majors was bigger than life and had been the rock not only for her sons, but for much of the community as well.

This was just a temporary illness, we all thought. It would pass. It had to. In deference to me, she had put off exploratory surgery until I could come home and take her to the Columbus, Ohio hospital where doctors would perform an open biopsy to obtain a tissue sample for diagnosis by the Mayo Clinic. On the 21st of December, I watched over my mother's shoulder as she signed the hospital's release and consent form on which she added, "Permission not granted to remove left leg." In her heart, she knew. I sat next to my mother as we waited for her room and she fell asleep in a chair. She looked so tired from the cares of life.

A week later, after the surgery had gone well, we all celebrated Christmas in the hospital. I flew back to California and no sooner had my head hit the pillow than the phone began to ring. It took me some time to shake myself awake.

I stumbled out of the bedroom and fell over the suitcases I had left in the middle of the living room as I searched for the phone. I glanced at the clock. It was 5:30 a.m. California time, December 28. I'd been asleep four hours.

"Hello?" I answered.

I heard the voice of my older brother, Franklin, on the other end of the line. "Hi, Sam," he said. "I have some bad news." He hesitated. "Mom passed away this morning."

"What? Oh, no. I'm so sorry," I heard myself say without emotion, as if I were offering condolences to some distant acquaintance. To this day, I find it odd that I reacted with such detachment about someone I loved so much.

My brother went on to tell me that a state trooper had come knocking on his door several hours earlier—it was 8:30 a.m. in Ohio—to give him the bad news. Apparently, the nurse had been putting Mom back to bed after helping her in the bathroom, and suddenly she gasped and then stopped breathing. He tried to resuscitate her, but without success.

Slowly, reality began to sink in as a numbness swept over me that cannot be described. One has to experience it personally. It wasn't someone else's mother who had died; it was my mother. She was dead, and it was final. Mom was gone and she wasn't coming back, I had to keep telling myself.

"Are you going to have an autopsy performed?" I heard myself ask Frank. Yes, there would be an autopsy. Frank would call our eldest brother, Marshall, in Cleveland, and I would call Dad and my mother's secretary, Freema Glick. Frank would pick me up at the airport.

I dialed my father's number back in Ohio and waited as it rang. I began hoping I was having a bad dream from which I was going to wake up at any moment.

"Hello?" my father answered sleepily. At the age of 71, he felt he'd earned the right to sleep late.

"Dad, this is Sam. I've got some bad news. Mom passed away this morning."

"What?" he exclaimed in shock and disbelief.

I repeated myself.

"What happened?" he asked.

"I don't know much yet. Frank just called me. I have to call to make flight arrangements. He is going to pick me up at the airport tonight."

As we talked, I could sense the wheels turning in his head. At long last, justice had been served. The lucrative law practice that my father believed my mother had stolen from him would now be his. "I gotta go now, Dad. I'll call you when I get in tonight."

I next dialed my mother's secretary, Freema Glick. I hoped Freema would still be at home since my mother's law office didn't open until 9:00 a.m.

Freema Glick was to my mother what Della Street had been to Perry Mason. Competent, efficient, and above all, fiercely loyal. My mother had brought Freema with her in 1967 when she left the bench after losing her bid for reelection during my parents' divorce. Freema had helped Mom start her practice and had remained with her for nineteen years with the exception of a brief time during which Freema decided to "retire." In 1986, Mom persuaded her to come back to work. When Mom got sick, Freema virtually ran the office. All she lacked was the framed piece of paper on the wall.

Freema's husband, Howard, answered the phone. I explained what had happened and he went to get Freema. When she came on the line, I again explained the events as I knew them. Choking back tears, she cried, "This is tragic. I just talked to her last night. I was going to drive to the hospital tomorrow to bring her home and we were going to set up a little office at the house." I tried to console Freema the best I could, and we hung up.

Much of what happened the rest of the day was a blur. I remember waking my roommates to tell them what had happened and that I had to go home again. One of them commented that I was going to be set for life. I couldn't believe his callousness.

A good friend drove me to the airport. I thought the airline I had flown on the night before would surely give me a discounted fare in light of what had happened. Despite my explanation, the agent insisted she had to charge full price which came to over $800.

I couldn't believe it, but I had no choice. I handed her my credit card.

It was still the holiday season. As I walked through another airport to catch my connecting flight, I felt like I was moving in slow motion as I watched everyone's happiness in stark contrast to my sorrow—families talking and laughing while my pain was so great. This just couldn't be happening, but it was.

During the flight, my mind went back to my conversation with my mother just prior to her surgery. Choking back emotion, I said, "Mom, I want to thank you for all the sacrifices you've made for me."

"Oh, Honey," she replied, "it wasn't a sacrifice, it was my privilege."

"If it turns out you're really sick, I'm going to come back home to help you," I said.

"Oh, no, Honey. You're just getting started out there and I wouldn't want you to do anything to jeopardize that. Remember, 'to thine own self be true, then thou canst not be false to any man'." Her uppers must have been loose because, as she paraphrased Shakespeare, her eyes got big when her dentures almost flew out of her mouth. We had a good laugh, but, true to form, she had not thought of herself.

The plane listed violently back and forth as we descended to land at the Columbus airport during a blinding snow squall. Rather than being afraid, I wished at the time that the plane would crash so that my nightmare would end. Looking back, I am amazed I could be so selfish, but, when you're hurting, it's hard to think of anyone else.

The two-hour ride with Franklin through the cold and snowy darkness to our hometown of Friendly, Ohio, was uneventful. Neither of us had much to say as we were both still in shock. Marshall was waiting for us, having arrived several hours earlier. It seemed surreal to come home to the house without Mom there. As I trudged up the front walk where Marshall had cleared a small path through the snow, *I wondered to myself how Mom would have shoveled herself out had she been alive.*

As I walked in the front door, I wanted to yell, "Hi, Mom, I'm home!" as I always had, and to hear her answer exuberantly, "Hi, Honey!" It didn't seem right to walk into the family room and not find her stretched out on the couch nursing one of those unfiltered Camel cigarettes she liked to smoke right down to the nubbins as she had since she was 15. Invariably, she would be wearing one of her dirty old house dresses and a pair of ratty old angel tread slippers as she watched "Wheel Of Fortune." But now the house was quiet. Mom had acquired a new set of angel treads.

The morning after our mother's death, Marshall went to Mom's office early to review her Last Will and Testament. Marshall was a graduate of Harvard Law School. A tenacious litigator best described as a shark with a conscience, Marshall practiced the art of selective feeding; he always tried to be ahead of the game.

Franklin and I arrived an hour later and walked in as Freema was taking her coat off. The purpose of our meeting was to discuss what was going to happen to our mother's law practice.

Franklin was the middle child. Also an Ivy League law grad, he had always lived in the shadow of our older brother, Marshall, with whom he was forced to compete from Day One. I, on the other hand, had always been the underachiever, and had chosen to attend a small law school in the Bible Belt. After law school, I earned a Master's in Communication and had produced local television news for several years before moving to California.

I had always been happy to coast along on my parents' and older brothers' reputations. It wasn't until I failed the bar exam on my first try that I finally knew what it meant to have to make it on my own merits. Though Mom had always told me I had more native ability than my two older brothers, I had never believed her.

Mom's law office was located on the third floor of a downtown bank building that was well over 100 years old. It was the same building where our parents had opened their first law office after Dad came home from World War II. Their apartment was on the floor directly above their law office and Mom told me she used to stomp on the floor to let my father know when dinner was ready. Years later, after my father had moved his office to another building, the apartments on the third floor were converted to offices. Ironically, when my mother started her law practice after the divorce, she ended up renting the same three rooms in which she had first set up housekeeping.

Marshall, Frank and I were seated in the conference room around the antique oak dining table I had refinished for my mother. I sat across from Freema, whose eyes were still red from crying. Because Mom had been the Dower County Probate

Judge, and something of a woman's pioneer, she had developed a very lucrative probate practice after she left the bench—especially among some of Friendly's wealthier elderly widows.

Marshall had Mom's Last Will and Testament in his hand. After a careful search in all the secure locations, he had found it lying open on top of the office safe. With things in the office being so unsettled, apparently Freema hadn't noticed it lying there.

Before I took Mom to the hospital, she had apparently taken her Will out for review. I couldn't help but think it strange that she had tossed such an important document on top of the safe in such a casual, haphazard fashion. As Mom hurriedly left the office to go to the hospital, had she sensed time was short, or had she believed she would soon be back? Whatever the case, before she left, she had asked Freema to stay and help me if anything happened to her and I came back to take over the practice, and Freema promised Mom she would.

Mom's Will was relatively straightforward. "I, Margaret Majors, being of sound mind and memory, give, devise and bequeath all of my property, both real and personal, of whatsoever kind and wheresoever situate, in equal shares to my three sons, Marshall R. Majors, Franklin B. Majors and Samuel E. Majors. I appoint my eldest son, Marshall, to serve as my Executor."

As if on cue, the phone began ringing. Marshall answered it. It was one of my mother's elderly clients. After a moment, Marshall turned the speaker phone on so we could all hear the elderly woman's voice, "But what about my Last Will and Testament? Your mother agreed to hold the original. What's going to happen to all of my papers now that she's gone?" she asked with concern.

Without missing a beat, Marshall answered, "You have nothing to worry about, ma'am. Everything is just as it was when our mother was alive and we're going to make sure all of her clients are well taken care of. As Margaret Majors' oldest son, you have my word on it."

The woman sniffled. "I hope so. I certainly did love your mother."

"Thank you, Ma'am. We all did. We'll be sending you a letter very soon letting you know what our plans are," he told her reassuringly as she hung up the phone.

Marshall looked over at me. "That's the third call this morning."

"I can't believe it," I said in disgust. "She's barely been dead 24 hours. What do they think...that we've got a fire going out in the back alley and we're burning all their files?"

"No brother," Marshall answered gently. "They're just worried." He hesitated. "But you're going to have to make a decision."

"A decision? Me? What are you talking about?" Silly me. I had no idea where this was going.

"About whether you're going to come back from California to take over Mom's practice," Marshall answered.

"Me? Why me?" I exclaimed in my little brother mode. "You're both lawyers. Why don't one of you come back and take it?"

"I can't leave the firm in Cleveland after they just made me a partner, and Frank isn't going to give up his seat in the state legislature, are you Frank?" Frank shook his head in the negative.

"Then that leaves you, Sam. It's a helluva practice. A once-in-a-lifetime opportunity! Mom had one of the most lucrative probate practices in town."

"But what about my life in California?" I cried.

"What was it you were doing out there?" Marshall asked, trying to remember, as if he had ever really known or cared. "Working as a paralegal at Columbia Pictures," I replied. "Oh, yeah," he acknowledged flatly.

"But that was just to pay the bills," I said. "I just pitched a pilot last week to one of the networks and I'm waiting to hear their response."

Marshall shrugged, unimpressed. "Well, it's your life. No one is forcing you to come back. But if you don't, in a few weeks, it'll all be gone. You can see that already. I'll sell Mom's house, wind up the practice, and that'll be it. You can go back to Hollywood and pursue your dream. Maybe you'll make it, maybe you won't."

An air of resignation hung heavy over my head. The thought of pushing a shopping cart down Hollywood Boulevard with all my worldly belongings in it wasn't too appealing.

"How much does it cost to run the practice?" I asked.

"About $5,000," Freema said.

That's not too bad, I thought to myself.

Then she added, "That's $5,000 per month."

"Where would I get that kind of money?" I asked in desperation.

Without hesitating, Marshall offered to have the estate pay all the expenses, and let me keep all the fees.

"But it's been nearly 10 years since I was admitted to the Bar. And I've never really practiced law," I said, still searching for a way out.

"That wouldn't be a problem. Freema worked with Mom for nearly 20 years. There's nothing Mom hasn't taught her," Marshall said.

"Don't look at me," Freema replied. "I'm no lawyer. I don't know why you're all so concerned now, anyway. Your mother is dead. Why weren't any of you here when she really needed you?"

Ouch. That hurt. Good old Freema. She always had the ability to cut through all the pleasantries and get right to the point.

"None of us expected Mom to die, Freema. But she's gone now and we can't bring her back, so we have to make the best of it," Marshall replied. "Won't you consider staying, at least temporarily, to help out Sam?" Marshall asked.

"But what about all of Mom's pending cases?" I asked, feeling like a mountain climber quickly losing ground in a rockslide.

"Hoping you might agree to stay on temporarily, I asked Victor Faircloth if he would meet with us to talk about helping make the transition," Marshall replied. He had thought of everything. Victor Faircloth was an up-and-coming probate attorney whom Mom had mentored, as she had done with so many others. Mom and Victor's mother had been friends for many years. When Franklin wanted to attend prep school after our parents' divorce, it was Mrs. Faircloth who arranged for a scholarship. And when one of Mrs. Faircloth's other sons needed guidance as a teenager, it was Mom who helped him back on the straight and narrow. Best of all, Freema was one of Victor's biggest fans.

Unbeknownst to any of us, Freema, along with Victor's mother and Mom's best friend, Ruth Duryea, had quietly been lobbying Mom to make Victor her partner. Over the years, Mom had been approached many times with similar opportunities, but had always told the would-be suitors, "No, I am saving the practice in case one of the boys wants to come back." Had Mom not died so suddenly and unexpectedly, I suspect this latest lobbying effort might have succeeded.

Just then there was a knock at the door. It was Victor Faircloth. Marshall moved swiftly to make his pitch. In exchange for helping me get started, some sort of arrangement would be made, perhaps an equity interest in Mom's practice. Marshall had researched the ethics of selling a law practice. It couldn't be done under Ohio law because of client confidentiality, but Mom's attorney-client relationship could be continued with me subject to the client's consent.

Victor and Freema exchanged glances. He seemed receptive, and thought some sort of arrangement could be worked out. He'd have to give it some thought. Our meeting ended and my brothers and I left to make arrangements with the town's only funeral director, Maple Grove.

CHAPTER 2

Maple Grove could best be described as the Danny DeVito of undertakers, the two bearing a striking resemblance in appearance and personality. Maple's funeral home was not the best funeral home in Friendly; it was the only funeral home in Friendly. He also owned a cemetery that bore his name.

The Maple Grove Funeral Home was located in an old Victorian mansion two blocks down from Mom's office. It had endured a number of changes through the years so that it only slightly resembled its former grandeur. The interior decor could best be described as respectably trashy, the Victoria's Secret of funeral homes.

After knocking the snow off our shoes, we were ushered into a small room off the entry hall, while one of Maple's minions went to summon him from the embalming room. Tastefully displayed on every square inch of wall space surrounding us were grave markers, memorials and various examples of ways to remember your loved one. I especially liked the one that allowed you to hear a pre-recorded message from the dearly departed simply by pushing a button on the grave marker located next to their picture.

After what seemed like an eternity, Maple entered the room. He extended his hand to Marshall but suddenly drew back when he realized he had forgotten to remove the yellow rubber gloves he wore while embalming.

Maple was appropriately sympathetic, lavishing praise on our mother, telling us what a wonderful person she had been.

Truth be told, Mom had confided to me that he had appeared before her on several occasions as a juvenile when she was Judge. In one case, he and some other teenage boys had used a straightedge razor to shave all the pubic hair off a willing high school cheerleader. In another case, Maple and his father had been arrested for drag racing down Main Street. Is it possible that a man Maple's age can be 50 and still be a juvenile delinquent? In Maple's case, it was.

There was a story around town that Maple had gotten his name because he was conceived on his parents' kitchen table after a hearty breakfast of pancakes and sausage.

Marshall handed Maple our mother's *curriculum vitae* for the obituary. It must have been 20 pages long. If there was a civic organization or board to serve on, Mom had done it. But above all, she always said that her most important accomplishment was raising us boys. We had been her life. That is why, when Maple asked what we wanted inscribed on her stone, Marshall's voice broke as he said, "She was a mother." Actually, I had been the one who had supplied that little piece of information to Marshall before our visit to the funeral home.

Mom's parents were buried in a mausoleum in eastern Ohio near the small mining community in which she had been raised, and where she wanted to be buried as well. Quite often on our trips back there to visit my grandmother when I was young, we would stop at the mausoleum, and every time, she would tell me, "I don't care if you don't even put my name on the stone, I just want it to read, 'She was a mother.'" And so, in addition to her name and dates of birth and death, I made sure her request was honored.

After we got home from making the funeral arrangements, Marshall got a call from the doctor who had performed the autopsy. The cause of death was unmistakable. Mom had died from a pulmonary embolism. Essentially, a blood clot had broken loose when she was straining to go to the bathroom. When the male nurse lifted her legs into bed, it made its way to her lungs and killed her instantly.

When Marshall talked to the surgeon, he advised that he had not given her any Coumadin to prevent clotting because he anticipated having to amputate her leg in the near future. Had her blood been thinned, he reasoned, she might have hemorrhaged and died on the operating table. In his mind it was a matter of weighing the opposing risks.

In my mind, it was a matter of malpractice. If he had given her the Coumadin, would she still be alive? From my perspective, she had fallen through the cracks. This wonderful woman who was so important to so many people had died because of a bad call on the doctor's part. I was bitter. I wanted to sue. And while we might have had a case, Marshall decided against it because he didn't think Mom would want to have been remembered that way. He was probably right.

That night before we went to bed, a funny thing happened at the house. The toilets began gurgling and the shower backed up. The next morning, a plumber discovered the problem. Tree roots had plugged up the sewer.

"Ironic, isn't it," Frank observed, "Mom and the house both got plugged up at the same time."

CHAPTER 3

As I lay in bed that night, my thoughts drifted back to the day after Mom's surgery, which had taken place a week earlier. She was still in the hospital and I had driven back home to Friendly to celebrate Christmas Eve with Dad, as Marshall, Franklin and I had done ever since our parents' divorce. I was alone in the house that night. Marshall and Frank would arrive the next morning on Christmas Eve. I was trying to go to sleep when suddenly I felt the presence of death. I didn't understand the significance at the time, but looking back, I often wonder if I was visited by the angel of death who had come that night searching for my mother. That experience haunts me to this day.

The next few days after her death were a terrible blur. If you've ever lost a loved one unexpectedly, you know what I'm talking about.

Dad and I had agreed to meet for breakfast. He did not look well and I suspect Mom's death had shaken him more than he cared to admit. I don't believe the two of them had ever really gotten over the love they once had for each other.

After my parents divorced, Dad married a woman named Betty who bore a striking resemblance to our mother, but who presented no threat mentally and was 19 years younger. They had a son, Clayton, when Dad was 58 and Betty was 39. Now he was alone once again, having divorced his second wife. As he approached 75, Dad was trying to raise my 16-year-old half-brother alone, Betty having moved away in self-imposed exile.

Because Mom had been deeply hurt in her marriage and was a scrapper, she had earned the reputation of being one of the best divorce lawyers in town. She and Aaron Longworth, another attorney whose office was on the same floor of the bank, used to love to go at it in court like a couple of junk yard dogs fighting over a bone. They thrived on trying to outsmart each other. After a case was over though, they'd always go out and smoke a cigarette and have a beer together.

Eventually, the course of conversation with my father over breakfast that morning turned to me and my plans. When I had talked about moving to California several years earlier, Dad had been the one to encourage my dreams of working in television. But now, he seemed to be of a different opinion. When I told him Marshall wanted me to come back to Friendly to assume Mom's practice, I was surprised to hear him say he thought it was a good idea. "You could stay long enough to get established, and then you could go back," he said. "I'll be here to help you get started," he offered.

"But you know my heart is in California," I said. "You were the one who encouraged me to go out there in the first place."

"I know that, son," Dad replied with a great deal of empathy and understanding in his voice. "And I still feel that way," he continued, as he tried to be encouraging. "It may not seem like it now, but sometimes the indirect route is the fastest way to get to where you really want to go."

I wasn't satisfied. In my heart I knew that eventually he would get around to suggesting the merging of our practices, but I let the matter drop.

That afternoon, before the visitation at the funeral home, we were allowed in for some private moments with our mother. I was the first to arrive. Seeing Mom lying there in the casket brought tears to my eyes. I stroked her arm, kissed her on the cheek and thanked her again for all she had done for us.

I will say this for Maple, he did know his craft. Mom looked 10 years younger; all the worry and pain which had been on her face the week before were now gone. She was radiant.

That night, despite the cold and the snow, people waited in line several hours to pay their respects. One of the first through the door was Mom's good friend and client, Ruth Duryea, Victor Faircloth's biggest fan. She had run one of the fashionable clothing shops in Friendly during the time Mom had been Judge and was probably worth several million dollars. As soon as she arrived, Freema took her by the arm and led her over to the casket. In the course of conversation, I mentioned that our plumbing had backed up. Ruth offered, in fact she insisted that I come over and let her do my laundry. Never one to turn down the kindness of strangers, I accepted.

I couldn't count the number of other clients that night who said, "She wasn't just my attorney, she was my friend." What better tribute could an attorney have? Many related how proud she was of my brothers and me and how often she spoke of us— especially of me. It was very moving.

Next day's memorial service played to a packed house at the church. Nearly every attorney from the Dower County Bar Association showed up to honor our mother—except, of course, for our father. Someone later told me they overheard several attorneys talking as they left the memorial service about how Mom's practice was going to be carved up.

That afternoon I went to Ruth's house to drop off my dirty laundry. After we talked about the service, Ruth began relating how lonely Mom had been the last year of her life, and how she would come over every morning before she went to the office to have toast and coffee. At one point she gestured to an easy chair in the corner of the living room and told me how Mom had kept a pair of her slippers under it. I couldn't find it in my heart to ask if they were still there.

I was still undecided about what I should do, so I asked Ruth's advice. After hearing me relate how torn I was about the situation, she waved her hand with an air of dismissal, and said, "Go back. Go back to California. Your mother wouldn't want you to stay here if she thought you were going to be unhappy."

True enough, but the way she said it left me somewhat puzzled. Wasn't this Mom's best friend? Surely she must have known our mother had hoped one of us would one day take over her practice. Then why was she so anxious to have me return to California? Whether she knew it or not, Ruth's eagerness to have me leave Friendly for good played a role in my decision to stay.

Later, I was to discover that when Freema called Ruth to tell her Mom had died, she had picked up all her files from the office. Undoubtedly, Freema had called her as soon as she had hung up after talking to me. My mother wasn't even cold before Ruth had changed allegiances. Actions like Ruth's, of people to whom Mom had been especially close, puzzled and hurt me.

December 31, 1988, was a very sad, very lonely New Year's Eve without Mom. The next morning, New Year's Day, Marshall, Franklin and I made a long silent trip to cold and snowy eastern Ohio where Mom had been born seventy-one years before.

Mom's father had worked in a coal mine and she had grown up in a small village on the edge of the Appalachian mountain range. Even with the cover of snow, the place looked pretty bleak.

Maple was there waiting for us at the mausoleum when we arrived, with our mother lying in an open, cold casket. The structure was a large, unheated, 100-year-old Gothic marble edifice built in a cemetery where several generations of my mother's family had been buried. Two long walls of crypts faced each other. They were stacked four vertically, one on top of the other, and spanned 30 across. We entered through a massive steel and glass door. It was so cold we could see our breath.

A crypt on the bottom at one end away from all of my mother's relatives was standing open. It was the only one available. On the other end of the mausoleum at the top, there was an unused crypt next to my grandmother's, but we were told it already belonged to someone. Just then, one of my mother's cousins who owned the crypt showed up for the internment ceremony and offered to sell it to us. Mom would get to be next to her mother after all. It was a bittersweet ending to a very sad time.

Late that afternoon back in Friendly, Franklin and Marshall left to return to their busy lives, leaving me alone in Mom's big empty house, for what appeared to be my destiny—to continue the work of my mother's life. The house was filled with all the flowers the funeral home had delivered. Since I was freezing, my body having become accustomed to the warm California winters, I decided to start a fire in the fireplace. Winters in Ohio are characterized by a five-month period of grey skies where one seldom sees the sun—such a contrast to the place I had left behind filled with warmth and light.

As I stood there trying to stoke the coals, anger and bitterness swept over me. I stamped my foot and raised my hand in anger. Why, God, had you allowed this to happen to me? Why? I had felt wonderfully free in California for the first time in my life, pursuing my dreams, answering to no one. Now I had a feeling that a prison door was slowly closing shut on me. I felt trapped.

CHAPTER 4

The next morning I needed some cash, so I stopped by the Buckeye Savings Bank located below Mom's office with my last paycheck from Columbia Pictures. There were several tellers, but one in particular caught my eye. She was young and very pretty—with dark hair, beautiful chestnut brown eyes, and olive skin.

As I waited in line, everyone seemed to be staring at me with a look of judgment on their faces. Was I imagining things?

I had been gone from Friendly a long time. I tried to smile at several people, but they turned away. A look, a gesture, some went out of their way to make sure I knew I was an outsider.

White ... Anglo Saxon ... even Protestant. And this was my hometown. So what was their problem? If you've ever moved to a small provincial town, especially one surrounded by cornfields and a history of isolation, you know what I'm talking about.

The line slowly inched forward. Finally, it was my turn. The next available teller appeared to be an 80-year-old lady badly in need of a diarrhetic. Her face was drawn up into a terrible knot, most likely because the bun on her head had been twisted one turn too many. Her name plate read Minerva Weasel, but I thought, *"Old Prune Face" would have been a better moniker.* As she glowered at me, I thought maybe a little humor might brighten her day. As I sauntered up to her window, I asked, "Did you hear about the dwarf fortune teller who robbed a bank?" The old lady's eyes grew wide. I continued, "The newspaper headline read, 'Small Medium at Large.'"

I heard the other teller snicker and suddenly, Ms. Weasel placed a sign in her window which read, "This Window Closed." I stepped back, relieved, when a customer left the window of the other teller whom I really wanted to meet.

A new kind of apprehension swept over me, the kind you don't mind. She was beautiful. As I moved closer, I could read her nameplate: Tori Epstein. This situation was improving by the moment.

"Hi," I said. "I'm Sam Majors."

"I know," she replied nonchalantly. "Your mother was my Great Aunt's attorney."

"She was? What a small world," I said self-consciously. *What a stupid cliche*, I thought to myself. Why did I say that? Now she was bound to agree with everyone else in the bank lobby.

I pushed my check across the counter. She picked it up and her eyes got big. "You work for Columbia Pictures?"

"I do. I mean I did, until I took a leave of absence. I mean, could I cash this please?"

"My Great Aunt used to work for Columbia Pictures back in the 1930's. She was a contract player."

"She was?" I asked excitedly. "What was her name?"

"Sarah Singleton," Tori replied.

"She starred in *Always the Bridesmaid and Never the Bride!*"

Tori nodded, smiling, "Yes, I believe that was one of her pictures."

"I just saw it last month at a film festival in Santa Monica! She was great." My confidence was beginning to return.

"What did you do at Columbia Pictures? Are you an actor?" Tori inquired.

"No, I was working in their legal department, but that was just my day job. What I really want to do is write for network television. I just pitched a pilot to one of the networks a couple of weeks ago."

"You did?" her eyes got wide. "How exciting!"

Suddenly we both became aware that "Old Prune Face" was staring at us disapprovingly. Tori excused herself momentarily to get the manager's approval to cash my check because I didn't have an account and it was from an out-of-state bank.

I fidgeted nervously while I waited. It felt like the eyes of everyone in that lobby were burning holes through me.

After the manager sized me up from a distance and whispered something to Tori, she returned and proceeded to process my check.

As Tori counted out and handed me the cash, our fingers touched briefly. That wonderful moment was suddenly interrupted by several loud blasts from a can of air followed by the ringing of a bicycle bell and the putt-putt-putt of a motor.

I turned to see an elderly man with silver hair, clad in a three-piece suit, astride a moped complete with basket and streamers, riding through the crowded bank lobby screaming, "There's a run on the bank! There's a run on the bank! Quick, get your money." People were laughing and pointing. The old man whizzed past me yelling as he rode toward the exit. "There's a run on the bank! A run on the bank! Quick get your money." He faded away.

"Who was that?" I asked as I turned back to Tori in amazement.

"That?" Tori replied, unfazed. "Oh, that was just Aaron Longworth."

"Aaron Longworth, the attorney?"

Tori nodded, her eyes twinkling as she smiled.

So this was the guy Mom had always done battle with? I didn't know it at the time, but Aaron's son, Neville, was next in line directly behind me, listening to us and watching my every move. He cleared his throat loudly. Tori's smile faded ever so slightly.

"You've got other customers. I'd better go. Be seein' ya," I said.

"I hope so," Tori whispered back.

I moved down to another place to count my money, but my ears pricked up at what I heard Tori say to her next customer. I pretended to examine a bank promotion as I tried to eavesdrop.

"What was all that about?" Neville demanded.

"Don't ask me. How should I know why your father rides his moped through the bank," Tori replied.

"You know what I'm talking about. That guy you were talking to," Neville said as he motioned at me over his shoulder with his thumb.

"Who? That guy?" Tori asked innocently. "He was just a customer. Remember? I work here."

"Just a customer?" Neville growled. "You flirt with all your customers that way?"

"Only the good looking ones," Tori retorted.

I smiled to myself. I had never thought of myself as particularly good looking—just average, I guess, but I was glad Tori thought differently. Actually, Neville and I couldn't have been more opposite in appearance.

While I was 5'10", about two inches taller than Tori, Neville was a good six inches taller than both of us. I always had a pretty good crop of brown hair, while Neville's, what was left of it, was salt and pepper grey. I doubted it would be long before he'd be a good candidate for a comb-over to cover the growing bald spot on top of his head.

While I was no Charles Atlas, I had done a pretty good job of keeping my medium build in relatively good shape. In Neville's case, though, it seemed as if the sands of time had shifted, leaving him looking like Ichabod Crane with a middle-aged paunch. Neville had a good ten years on both Tori and me. Was I going to look like that at his age? Not if I could help it.

Upstairs, I stepped off the ancient elevator onto the third floor. A sign on the wall had arrows pointing in the direction of the offices of Longworth and Longworth, where Neville and his father practiced law together when Neville wasn't serving as the Dower County Prosecuting Attorney. Another arrow pointed toward Mom's office and a third pointed toward Mark Tuttle's office, another young attorney whom Mom had taken under her wing.

When I burst into Mom's office, it was sometime after ten a.m. "Freema, you wouldn't believe what Aaron Longworth just did down in the bank!"

Freema was in the midst of a conversation on the telephone, and motioned for me to be quiet. She was always in control. "I've agreed to stay on temporarily for the sake of the clients. No, we're not accepting any new cases right now, but Margaret referred several cases to Mark Tuttle down the hall. He's a fine young attorney. All right, then. Thank you, and goodbye."

I slumped in one of the chairs sitting in the waiting area by Freema's desk, my confidence once again deflated. Freema looked at her watch and then up at me with an expression that indicated office hours did not begin at ten a.m.

"Who was that?" I asked weakly.

"Another of your mother's clients. Your mother handled two of her divorces, and now she wants another one. She says it will probably be contested so I referred her to Mark Tuttle down the hall."

Freema could sense my displeasure at her lack of confidence. "You don't think you're ready to take on an ugly contested divorce, do you?"

"No, I suppose not," I sighed with an air of resignation.

"Now what was it you just couldn't wait to tell me?" she asked.

"Huh? Oh, yeah. Aaron Longworth just rode his moped through the bank lobby screaming at the top of his lungs. Something about a run on the bank."

Freema shook her head in amusement. "Sounds like he's up to his old tricks again."

"You mean he's done it before?" I asked in disbelief.

"Every time there's a full moon. He'll do anything for attention. He used to come down here all the time and bother your mother. One day he burst in on her while she was in conference with clients, kissed her on the mouth, told her his friend out in Las Vegas had 17 whorehouses lined up and that he was going out there and get syphilis, bring it back, and give it to her."

"You're kidding! What did she do?" I asked through my laughter.

"Nothing. It took a lot to faze your mother."

Freema continued, "One day I was getting off the elevator with my son as Aaron was getting on. I said, "Mr. Longworth, I'd like you to meet my son." With a look of serious concern, he grabbed my arm and asked, 'He isn't ours, is he?' I could have died."

I was laughing so hard that for a moment I actually relaxed. I began to take my coat off when Freema stopped me. "You can leave your coat on. If you're going to be staying in Friendly, I think we should make a trip out to the nursing home so you can meet some of your mother's clients."

Meanwhile, down at the offices of Longworth and Longworth, Neville was fuming. Aaron was busy feeding baby toads to his aquarium full of piranha which he kept in his personal office. His moped was resting against the wall. Neville paced back and forth like a caged lion as he talked to his father. "But you said, and I quote, 'Margaret Majors' practice is going to fall into our lap like a ripe plum off the tree.'"

With an edge in his voice that could cut steel, Neville read aloud a notice Marshall had placed in that morning's edition of the Dower County Crier, "We are pleased to announce the continuation of the law practice of Margaret Majors by her youngest son, Samuel P. Majors, who has recently returned to Friendly from the West Coast."

Neville threw the paper down in a fit of rage. "That doesn't sound like much of a ripe plum to me." Aaron didn't move a muscle. He was busy communing with nature. He loved those fish; they were a great source of inspiration.

Slowly his eyes began to narrow. "Hmmm—" he mused. "Well?" Neville demanded.

Aaron's frown slowly changed to a grin, a very evil grin. He chuckled wickedly as he dropped another toad into the water and watched the hungry piranha close in for the kill. "Just give it some time, my boy, just give it some time. It may take a little longer, but it will happen."

CHAPTER 5

Freema and I turned onto Harmony Lane, the street on which Buckeye Manor nursing home was located. I was driving Mom's recently acquired Cadillac. She had been so proud of that car. After years of doing without so as to educate her three sons, owning a Cadillac made her feel like she had finally arrived.

Actually, her late model used car had been a gift from my uncle because she would never have been that extravagant on herself. I'm not sure whether she was more proud of the car itself, or of the fact that her brother had given her such a wonderful gift.

I slowed as we neared a curve. An addition was going up on the church located next to the nursing home. We passed a huge billboard that read:

Renaissance New Faith Tabernacle
Praise the Lord
We're growing with Jesus!
Rev. Virgil Freelander, Pastor

The billboard was dominated by a large likeness of Reverend Freelander holding a Bible in his hand outstretched toward the heavens and sporting a big toothy grin. Reverend Freelander's church had always had a legend surrounding it. Strange things were supposed to go on there.

Back in the 1950's, it had been a small struggling fundamentalist congregation located across town on the "other side of the tracks." Reverend Freelander had arrived in Friendly for a revival pulling a small trailer behind his 1955 Nomad Station Wagon filled with his appropriately submissive wife and six children. He never left.

What Reverend Freelander lacked in education, he made up for in energy and charisma. Aided by the Jesus movement in the 1960's and 1970's and the Reagan prosperity, Reverend Freelander had managed to grow the congregation of that little church into quite a following. His was a loyal flock to whom he could do no wrong.

Now God had spoken to him. It was time to rise up and build a new cathedral to the Glory of God. Conveniently, one of his elderly parishioners had willed him 30 acres located next to the nursing home in which she lived. Reverend Freelander was a frequent visitor there, often calling upon his "senior saints" as he liked to call them, as well as anyone else with whom he could obtain an audience.

We rounded the curve, and Buckeye Manor came into view. It was a stately old Victorian mansion with a large circular drive in front. The spotty remnants of the last recent snow still covered the ground. A sign at the entrance gates read:

Buckeye Manor Nursing Home
A Fun Place to Be

The nursing home, still festooned for the holidays, was dwarfed by a giant inflatable snowman held aloft by several large air blowers tethered to the ground. With his huge grinning white head bobbing around in the wind, the three-story figure reminded me of the giant StayPuft Marshmallow Man who attempted to destroy New York in *Ghostbusters*.

The interior of the nursing home was still decked out for the Christmas season. Angels, Santas, Christmas-themed scenes of all kinds lined the halls and filled the foyers. Right now it was snack time, and nursing home aides Willie Ames and Audrey Harper were working the halls.

Willie was a greasy-haired lowlife who never got beyond the 10th grade. He had answered two help wanted ads: Buckeye Manor and Fred's Texaco. He had taken this one because he figured it would be less stressful than pumping gas. He hadn't bargained on the bed pans.

Audrey, on the other hand, loved her work and considered it her mission to help alleviate the suffering of the elderly. A very religious young woman, she was one of Reverend Freelander's most devoted handmaidens. She was also very pregnant and unmarried, but that was another story.

Willie was pushing an antique tea cart that squeak-squeak-squeaked with every turn of its oversized wooden wheels while Audrey gave each resident what she called, "A Little Taste of Heaven." This was the brand name of the fruitcake made and sold by Waldo Pride, who also happened to be the brother of the nursing home's owner, Muffie Welsh. It was the only snack Buckeye Manor served to its residents.

Pursuant to nursing home policy, Audrey was wearing her standard issue yellow rubber gloves. As she and Willie rounded a corner, they were nearly mowed down by Reverend Freelander who was at the nursing home calling on his flock.

"Well, Praise the Lord, if it isn't Audrey and Willie!" Reverend Freelander exclaimed in his fast West Virginia accent. Just like on the billboard, he was carrying his thick, leather-bound King James Bible. With his Cheshire cat grin, pompadour hairdo, boisterous voice and overpowering personality, he easily could have passed for a used car salesman.

Willie turned away and rolled his eyes while Audrey reached out to embrace her shepherd. "What a blessing to see you, Pastor Freelander!" Audrey gushed. "What are you doing here?"

"Just makin' a few house calls. Always have to be about the Lord's work, you know," Reverend Freelander proclaimed, as he helped himself to a piece of fruitcake off the cart.

"Yes, I know what you mean. I really feel God has called me here to minister to these dear old souls," Audrey replied with sincerity.

Reverend Freelander hugged her in a fatherly way as she beamed up at him, "That's my girl."

Willie saw what was coming next, but couldn't back up quick enough. Reverend Freelander grabbed his hand and began pumping. "Willie, when are we going to see you at church? God could really use a fine young man like you."

Willie retrieved his arm, wiping it on his pants unconsciously. "Uh, I have to work on Sundays. Besides, I'm Catholic."

"Well, Praise the Lord anyways. You're always welcome! Gotta go now, kids. God bless you!" Reverend Freelander shouted over his shoulder from halfway down the hall.

Audrey called after him in deep admiration, "God bless you, Pastor!"

Reverend Freelander paused at the door of one of his flock to pull his vest down. "Well, Praise the Lord, it's Sister Titus!" he shouted as he disappeared into her room.

"Isn't he wonderful," Audrey sighed.

Willie wasn't there to answer. He had already moved on to one of the TV lounges where Mr. Nofzinger was catnapping in front of the television. He had been watching the scene from *Arsenic and Old Lace* where the two old maids tell their horrified nephew how they do away with elderly gentlemen. Willie stood there enjoying the movie until Audrey arrived.

Although it was only late morning, Mr. Nofzinger already had his six o'clock shadow. He was wearing old worn slippers, a plaid flannel shirt and sweat pants held up by suspenders. His sunken jaw revealed he was not wearing his dentures.

Audrey bent down by his one good ear. "Mr. Nofzinger—Mr., Mr. Nofzinger—" Audrey called as she gently tried to shake him awake. "Mr. Nofzinger—" Audrey called again.

Growing impatient, Willie reached over and snapped one of Mr. Nofzinger's suspenders. "Hey, Pops. Wake up!" Poor Mr. Nofzinger awoke with a start.

"Willie, that was mean!" Audrey scolded, as she tried to comfort the disoriented old man. "I have half a mind to write you up!" Willie shrugged, amused by his prank.

"I'm sorry to have to wake you, Mr. Nofzinger, but it's snack time!" Audrey said in her best bright and cheery voice.

Mr. Nofzinger sat back in his chair and folded his arms defiantly. "What are we having?" he asked with childlike belligerence.

Willie picked up a silver tray laden with pieces of fruitcake and thrust it under his nose. "Here, Pops! Have A Little Taste Of Heaven!"

"Willie, your gloves!" Audrey exclaimed as she pointed to the pair lying on top of the tea cart. Willie sighed as he set the tray down and stretched the yellow rubber gloves on as tightly as possible, seeming to take delight in snapping the end of every finger.

Mr. Nofzinger looked up at Audrey pathetically, "Not fruitcake again. I'm gonna spit up if I have to eat any more of that shit!"

Willie stuck a piece in his own mouth. "It's not so bad, Pops."

"Try eatin' it three times a day, 365 days a year, and see how you like it then!" Mr. Nofzinger growled.

Audrey patted the old man on the shoulder. "Tell you what—I'll just leave a couple of pieces here on a napkin beside you. You don't have to eat them unless you get hungry."

Once out of Willie's earshot, Audrey leaned down and whispered in the old man's ear, "I'll try to bring you a Twinkie tomorrow." Audrey and Willie wheeled their squeaking cart down the hall leaving Mr. Nofzinger alone with the gummy confection. He looked at the fruitcake as he muttered with disdain. "A Little Taste of Heaven. Hmmmpf! Tastes more like it came from hell. Damn that Muffie Welsh makin' us eat this crap."

Mr. Nofzinger again looked down at the fruitcake that was sitting next to a Buckeye Manor brochure featuring an air-brushed picture of Muffie Welsh on the cover. With an impish gleam in his eye, he picked up the brochure, placed the fruitcake between the pages, squeezed them tightly together and then replaced the brochure on the table with a look of great self-satisfaction.

As we pulled into the parking lot, I maneuvered Mom's car next to a delivery truck bearing this sign:

Waldo Pride's Deluxe Fruitcake
A Little Taste of Heaven

A sound of squealing tires came from the bottom of the circular drive. As Freema and I walked toward the front door, a flashy red Jaguar cut us off. The driver must have had the sun roof partially open because we could hear the blaring music of Right Said Fred's song, "I'm Too Sexy."

The driver had jet black hair, wore dark glasses, a red hat and looked to be in her early fifties. She revved her engine a couple of times before she slid into her reserved parking space.

The car door opened and a pair of very shapely legs in stiletto heels planted themselves firmly on the pavement. She was wearing a form fitting dress which showed off all her curves, her walk communicating that she was aggressive and in control. Muffie acted as if she was unaware or even cared that anyone else was present as she headed toward the nursing home carrying a yappy little Shih Tzu. Later I learned that this was Rush, the nursing home's mascot.

Freema reached over to close my mouth which had dropped to the pavement. "Who's that?" I asked incredulously.

"That's Muffie Welsh," Freema replied with disgust. "She and her husband, Jack, own the nursing home." We watched Muffie do the fanny dance as she disappeared through the front door.

Not watching where I was walking, I stumbled over something on the sidewalk. Freema grabbed my arm, "Watch where you're going!" I looked down to see what I had tripped over.

It was a man working beside some seedlings planted along the sidewalk. It appeared the bark had been partially stripped away from the bottom of the young tree trunks.

I recognized the man immediately as Ronnie Trask, a mentally disabled individual with whom I had attended school until he had been channeled off into special education. He still had that nervous twitch in his right eye and those big buck teeth, which was why all the kids teased him so unmercifully. I am ashamed to admit I was one of them. Kids can be so cruel.

In elementary school, we used to call him "Ronnie the Retard." In junior high, we had grown a little more sophisticated, and so he became "Fishlips" because his teeth made his lips protrude. I wondered whether he still talked through his nose.

I had always secretly felt sorry for Ronnie. He lived with his grandparents who must have been poor because he came to school in worn dirty clothes which smelled bad. If you got close enough, you could see all the little blackheads that covered his face like pins on a map.

But now, Ronnie was all grown up and working at the nursing home. Like everyone else who was employed at Buckeye Manor, Ronnie was wearing yellow rubber gloves. It struck me as odd that he had a string of rabbit's feet hanging around his neck, similar to the ones we had worn on our belts for luck when we were growing up.

He was seated next to a large box bearing a skull and crossbones labeled "*Insta-Death* All Purpose Poison For Home and Garden."

"Poison? What are you using poison for?" I asked incredulously.

"Bunnies," Ronnie guffawed as he removed one of his gloves and pulled a handkerchief from his back pocket to wipe the sweat off his forehead. "Chew the bark off Mrs. Welsh's new trees during the winter." He hadn't lost his gift of nasal intonation.

"So she poisons them?" I asked dumbfounded as Freema pulled me along.

We entered through a grand old leaded-glass front door into the foyer, which Muffie had decorated in Victorian splendor for the holidays with a 20-foot Christmas tree. We had to pass the nurse's station, which I eventually came to refer to affectionately as "Checkpoint Charlie." The first person we encountered was Head Nurse Etta Swackhammer. She was no nonsense and all business, just Freema's type.

"Hi, Nurse Swackhammer," Freema exclaimed as we approached the head nurse's station. Nurse Swackhammer returned the cordiality, smiling at Freema until she saw me. "Hello," I said, nodding respectfully.

Freema signed the guest register that Nurse Swackhammer handed her after she had removed her yellow rubber gloves. "This is Margaret's son, Sam. I brought him out to meet some of his mother's clients," Freema said as she headed off down the hall.

I smiled at Nurse Swackhammer, but she remained stone-faced, watching me intently with that special Friendly look of judgment on her face. As I walked down the hall to catch up with Freema, I glanced back over my shoulder twice and each time Nurse Swackhammer was still staring at me with a look of suspicion. She gave me the willies. It was not until sometime later I would learn that she and Aaron Longworth were related by marriage.

Freema led me up the grand staircase and down one of the long halls that were part of the addition to the building you couldn't see from the street. The farther we walked into the nursing home, the louder it became—the ever present din of the intercom system ding-ding-dinging overhead followed by the continuous paging of the same personnel to different locations. *How did anyone ever get any rest here,* I wondered to myself. With the constant summoning of the same employees by name, it quickly became apparent to me that the facility was understaffed.

Freema hesitated at a door and knocked gingerly before entering. There were three names printed on three gold plaques beside the door. We were going to see Rachel McDowell.

The room was divided into three individual sleeping areas with curtains separating each bed. We passed two women who were asleep in their beds, each curled up in a semi-fetal position.

Freema cautiously peered around the third curtain. The woman whom I now assumed was Rachel was lying on top of her bed staring straight up at the ceiling. She was very neatly dressed in a pants and blouse, and wearing a furry rabbit's foot on a chain around her neck. *Maybe Ronnie had given it to her,* I thought to myself.

The bed rails were up on each side of the bed. A piece of uneaten fruitcake sat on the bedside table. With gentle entreaty, Freema called, "Rachel." Freema moved to the woman's bedside and took her hand in hers. Almost mechanically, Rachel turned her head to look at Freema.

"Rachel, it's Freema. Freema Glick. Margaret Majors' secretary."

Rachel smiled, "Oh, hello." Freema squeezed Rachel's hand lovingly.

Freema motioned me closer and put her hand on my arm. "Rachel, this is Margaret's youngest son, Sam. He is going to be taking over his mother's law practice."

"Oh, that's nice," Rachel said as she looked up at me. This sort of rapport with the elderly was new to me, but I tried to make conversation the best I could.

"Hello, Rachel. How are you today?" I asked as I shook her hand.

"Fine. I'm waiting for my daughter. She's coming to visit me this afternoon."

I pointed to a picture on Rachel's bedside table of a woman who must have weighed 500 pounds. "Is that her?" I asked.

"Uh, huh," Rachel nodded in childlike agreement. "That's my little Eunice."

"I hope you have a nice visit," I responded.

"Rachel, we'd better go now," Freema said, as she began pulling me away. "We have to visit some other clients."

I shook her hand gently as I left, "It was nice to meet you, Rachel."

"Thank you," she said. "I hope you'll come again."

"I will," I replied smiling.

As I left, Rachel turned her head back toward the ceiling in the same mechanical fashion as she had when we had entered.

"She seems like a nice lady. Does her daughter visit very often?" I asked Freema as we were walking down the hall.

Without breaking her stride, Freema replied, "Her daughter choked to death on a ham sandwich more than two years ago. Your mother settled her estate."

I grabbed Freema's arm. "Doesn't she know?" I asked.

"She may have known at one time, but she's lost all of her short-term memory. If you told her today, she'd have forgotten by tomorrow," Freema advised as she walked on ahead of me.

"How sad," I said to myself as I stood in the middle of the hall, gradually becoming more aware of the state of my clients' minds.

Freema had stopped at another doorway. "Are you coming?" she asked impatiently as I hurried to catch up with her.

As I peered through the doorway, I observed a very small wizened old lady with the curliest white hair I had ever seen. She was sitting in a wheelchair in a room all by herself with her back to us. In front of her was a walker with a pouch-like carrier on which she had sewn many pockets bulging with what I presumed were her treasures—a fly swatter, papers, a flashlight, Kleenex, etc.

"Who's that?" I asked in a whisper.

Freema pointed to the name plate by the door that read, "Opal Thomas." "You don't have to whisper. She's totally blind and can only hear out of one ear," Freema explained.

As we walked toward Opal, I could see over her shoulder that she was holding a furry rabbit's foot in one hand while she stroked it with the long bony fingers of the other. I wondered to myself how Ronnie decided which of the residents needed his good luck charm.

Opal was carrying on a very animated conversation with herself, but the words were inaudible. Freema bent down by her one good ear and put her hand on the woman's shoulder, "Opal." There was no response. "Opal," Freema called a little louder. Still no response. Freema switched ears. "Opal," Freema called again.

This time Opal sat upright in her wheelchair, shouting as older people with hearing loss sometimes do. "Huh? What? Is someone there?" Her voice was very shrill and high pitched.

"It's Freema Glick, Opal."

You'd have thought the woman was drowning, the way she grabbed hold of Freema. "Oh, Freema, it's so good of you to visit me," Opal cried. "I was just heartbroken when I heard about Margaret's death."

"It took us all by surprise, Opal. I have someone here I'd like you to meet," Freema said as she managed to wrestle free from Opal's iron-like grip and pull me over.

Opal reached out in desperation, "Freema? Freema?"

Somewhat reluctantly, I took Opal's hand. For a 90-year-old lady, her fingers held mine like a vise.

"Who's that?" Opal called.

I bent down by Opal's good ear. She had a body odor about her that I would come to learn is common among the elderly. "It's Sam, Opal. Sam Majors. I'm Margaret's youngest son."

Opal smiled, "Oh?" As she turned toward the direction of my voice, I could see that both pupils of her eyes were milky white.

Freema shouted, "He's going to be taking over Margaret's practice."

"Hello, Opal, it's nice to meet you," I said as I patted her arm. I was beginning to understand the role empathy had played in my mother's law practice.

Opal's eyes welled up with tears as she started to cry. "It's nice to meet you, Sam. Your mother was so good to me. I loved her so. I felt so bad when I couldn't go to her funeral."

I patted her arm again, "It's all right, Opal. I understand."

Just then, there was a knock at the door. Audrey walked in holding several slices of fruitcake on a napkin. She bent down by Opal's good ear. "I brought you some fruitcake, Opal."

"I have visitors now. Just set it down on the table, honey," Opal replied. Audrey did so and left the room.

Opal waited a few seconds and then asked, "Is she gone?"

"She's gone," I replied. Opal straightened up in her chair and pursed her lips. With puritanical propriety, she leaned forward and whispered in hushed tones what in her day would have been a scandal. "She's an unwed mother because she found out the hard way!"

"What's that?" I asked.

"A stiff pecker has no conscience!" Opal declared.

I had to bite my lip to keep from laughing. I looked at Freema who, of course, wasn't laughing and then at the fruitcake on the table next to Opal. "Opal," I asked, "do you have a sweet tooth?"

Opal giggled impishly, the moment of judgment passing as quickly as it had come. "Why, yes," she replied, "I do. How did you know?"

"Just a lucky guess. How would it be if I'd bring you some candy the next time I come to visit?"

A broad smile burst across Opal's face. "Oh, honey, thank you, thank you, thank you," Opal cried, as her eyes again filled with tears. She grabbed my hands, pulled them up to her mouth, and began kissing them repeatedly with rapid fire succession.

You'd have thought I'd given her a million dollars. "You're just like your mother. She was always bringing me goodies. I didn't know what I was going to do when she died, but now I feel so much better," Opal cried as she continued to kiss my hands.

I looked up at Freema with astonishment. Her face registered no response.

A few minutes later we were walking down another wing that housed independent living apartments for residents not yet ready for the nursing home.

"There is one more person I think you should meet," Freema said.

"Who's that?" I asked.

"Cora Merriweather. She's a retired schoolteacher."

"What did she teach?"

"Drama classes, I think."

"She must have retired before I made it to the high school, because I sure would have remembered a name like Merriweather. How many clients did Mom have out here, anyway?" I asked.

"It varies," Freema replied. "Right now there are three."

"These old people sure did love Mom, didn't they," I observed.

"They were her life," Freema responded.

"How often did she come out and visit them?"

"At least once a week," Freema replied.

I was surprised. I was only beginning to realize how much my mother had done for others.

Freema stopped at one of the apartments and knocked. The door, which was already ajar, swung open. Because the back of the couch faced the door, all we could see was the back of Cora Merriweather's gray-haired head over which cigarette smoke hung like a halo.

"Who is it?" she asked.

"It's Freema Glick, Cora, and I have Margaret's son, Sam, with me."

As I was to learn was often her custom, Cora slid her ashtray holding the lighted cigarette under the couch with her heel to hide the fact she had been smoking. How that woman failed to set herself or the nursing home on fire, I'll never know.

Cora stood up. I guessed her to be in her mid-eighties. She was tall and bore a striking resemblance to Elvira Gulch who terrorized Dorothy in *The Wizard of Oz*. She was politely formal and very proper, but not stuffy.

Cora greeted us warmly. "Hello, Freema, won't you please come in?" Freema led me through the door.

The apartment was furnished with 1930's art deco vintage antiques. The living room was combined with a kitchenette to the immediate right of the doorway. It had a small sink, a microwave built into the upscale cherry cupboards and a refrigerator located closest to the door where we had entered. A small kitchen table and chairs sat nearby. Through two open doors to my left, I could see her bedroom and bathroom, separated from the living room and kitchenette.

"Cora, I'd like you to meet Sam Majors."

"How do you do, Mrs. Merriweather, it's nice to meet you," I said, as we shook hands.

"It's Miss Merriweather, but please, do call me Cora."

I relaxed immediately. I knew I was going to like this lady.

"All right, then, Cora it is."

Cora motioned toward several chairs and we sat down. "It's so nice to finally get to meet you, Sam. Your mother has told me so much about you. I feel like we already know each other. I hear you're going to be taking over her practice."

"You did?" I asked.

"Good news travels fast," Cora replied, smiling. "You may not know it yet, but you're going to be a big success. If there's ever anything I can do to help you, just let me know."

"Thank you, Cora, I will, if you'll promise to do the same."

"Oh, I will," she chuckled. "I will." Something in her delivery gave me pause, but I let it go.

"We have a lot in common, you and I," Cora continued.

"Oh?" I asked curiously.

"Didn't your mother tell me you were trying to make it out in Hollywood?" Cora inquired.

"Well, yes, I am ... I mean, I was ..." I replied.

"I did the same thing when I was young," Cora said as she picked up a framed photograph from a table and handed it to me. It was a studio glamour shot from the 1930's.

And then it hit me. This was Tori's great aunt. "You wouldn't happen to have a niece who works in the bank would you?" I asked hopefully.

"Oh, have you met Tori?" Cora replied smiling. "I am her great aunt."

Bingo! What luck! "Just this morning she cashed my check," I said.

"Is this George Hurrell's work?" I asked as I examined the photograph.

Cora nodded. "I was a contract player for Columbia Pictures. Perhaps you heard of me—Sara Singleton? That was the name the studio gave me. I was cast as the girl who never got the man."

"*Always the Bridesmaid and Never the Bride?*" I asked excitedly.

Cora smiled, "Yes, that was one of my pictures. How did you know?"

"They screened it last month at a film festival in Santa Monica," I replied.

"One of my pictures? They screened one of my pictures?" Cora asked with delight. "I figured they'd given me up for dead."

"I never thought I'd get to actually meet a Columbia player, especially in Friendly, of all places!"

"Small world," Cora mused.

"But I thought Freema said your last name was Merriweather."

"That is my name," Cora replied. "I saw no point in keeping up pretenses after I came back to Friendly."

Suddenly and without warning, Cora's refrigerator started to make a horrible banging and thumping noise that ended with a terrible groan and a shudder.

"Quiet. Quiet in there!" Cora demanded.

"Is, is there something wrong with your refrigerator?" I asked hesitantly.

Cora quickly shot back, "I have a man in there and he keeps trying to get out."

The refrigerator began to bang a second time upon which Cora again shouted at it, "'Quiet,' I said, or I won't let you out! I've got company."

I looked at Freema in disbelief and then back at Cora. "You, you have a man in there and he keeps trying to get out?" I asked.

"Either that or my icemaker's on the blink again."

I started laughing. "Cora, I think we're going to be good friends."

Cora smiled, pleased her joke had amused. "I certainly hope so. I never had any sons, you know."

By now Freema was at the door. "We'd better be getting back to the office, Sam."

Cora and I stood up together and I walked around the couch. No sooner was my back turned to Cora than she let out a very loud, very wicked cackle. A chill went down my spine as she said, "Going so soon? I wouldn't dream of it. Why, my party's just beginning!" I stopped dead in my tracks, spun around and pointed at Cora as if we were playing charades. "The Wicked Witch of the West, the scene in the witch's castle, *The Wizard of Oz.*"

Cora chuckled as she whispered in my ear, "Come again when the boss'll let you stay longer. Promise?"

I shook Cora's hand and said with a smile, "Promise." After Cora had shut the door, I looked at Freema and laughed, "What a wonderful character!"

CHAPTER 6

The phone was ringing when Freema and I arrived back at the office. Freema fumbled with her keys momentarily, leaving them in the door, as she scrambled to answer the call. Mom and Freema had worked on such a shoestring in the early years that missing a call might mean missing a paycheck. Although it was now January 1989, it was still before cell phones, fax machines and e-mail had become commonplace.

"Hello? Margaret Majors' Office," Freema answered in her usually upbeat professional tone. "A person-to-person collect call. From whom?" Freema's face fell. "Yes, he's here. Just a minute," Freema mumbled. She handed me the receiver as I handed her the keys.

"Who is it?" I asked.

"A collect call from Hollywood," Freema responded flatly, as she picked up her purse. "Somebody named Marty."

My agent! At long last! My prayers had been answered. Maybe he was going to put an end to this nightmare and tell me the network loved my script and that I should catch the next flight out to L.A. I was so glad that I'd given him my number in Ohio.

"Yes, I'll accept the charges," I said without a moment's hesitation.

"Hey, Sammy boy, it's Marty!" he said in his thick Brooklyn accent. "How ya' doin'?"

For the moment, I forgot all about my problems. "Great, Marty, just great! Tell me you have good news. Did they like the script?"

Out of the corner of my eye, I could see Freema pretending not to eavesdrop.

"The floor was sticky, man!" Roughly translated, that means male network executives had been so excited by the project, they had ejaculated all over the floor. I know it's crude and sleazy, but then, that was my agent.

"So, do we have a deal?" I asked, almost unable to contain myself.

"Well, maybe," Marty replied.

"Well, do we or don't we?" I shouted. The suspense was killing me.

"That's why I'm callin', man," Marty responded. "I need an advance on my commission to do some major league schmoozing with these people."

What kind of agent needs an advance to wine and dine Hollywood players? The kind I had. He was the only one who had been willing to take me on as a client. Besides, his girlfriend worked in the story department at one of the networks and he had chutzpah.

"How much do you need?" I asked reluctantly.

"A couple hundred will probably do for now," Marty replied. "Spago ain't cheap!"

At least the door was still open. They hadn't rejected me outright.

"Remember, Sammy boy, it took Norman Lear five years and two pilots before "All in the Family" became a hit," Marty offered with his usual bravado.

True enough. Could I hope for as much? I was no Norman Lear, but I had nothing to lose, except money…and my dreams. In my mind, I didn't have a choice.

"I'll wire it to you tomorrow," I said. *That would give me another excuse to see Tori*, I thought to myself. I hung up, feeling cautiously optimistic.

Could a show like mine possibly succeed? It was different from anything on the networks in the late 1980's. Told in the style of Thornton Wilder's *Our Town*, I called my show *The Good Old Days*.

Set in a small town outside Detroit in 1917, *The Good Old Days* was about the turbulent times surrounding World War I, and the fictional Armstrong family of Flat Rock, Michigan, who use traditional family values to cope with the changing world around them.

The war, the airplane, the automobile, movies and radio, flappers, the women's suffrage movement and prohibition would provide some great story lines. Tying it all together would be Bill Armstrong, the recently deceased adult version of little Billy Armstrong in 1917, who comes back each week to introduce the show's theme and then wraps it up at the end with a few observations about the similarities between the good old days and modern times.

The show featured Bill's nostalgic visit back to times that were simpler. Best of all, it focused on a time period in American history that had never been dealt with in series fashion on network television. As a Mickey Rooney or Jonathan Winters type, Bill Armstrong would be a mischievous character people would enjoy watching.

In the pilot episode, the Armstrongs prepare to enter the automobile race at the Wayne County Fair so they can use the prize money to pay for five-year-old Betsy Armstrong's polio treatments. When her grandfather, Preston Armstrong, tries to check the gas tank with a lighted match, he accidentally blows up the family car. Everyone thinks all is lost until Henry Ford answers the Grandfather's letter in person and offers to let them use his famous race car. The family wins the big race and little Betsy Armstrong gets her much needed medical attention.

That was my idea—such as it was. When I shared it with Marshall, he sardonically characterized it as "Little House On Walton's Mountain." If the networks did happen to bite, I could always go back like Dad had said. If they didn't, well, at least I could say I had tried.

I looked at the clock. It was after five, and Freema had her coat on. It was time to close up shop. Just as we were about to turn off the lights, in walked Victor Faircloth. He arrived to inform me that he had thought it over, and that the counsel he had received made him decide against any formal association between us. Victor advised he would help me clean up Mom's pending cases on an hourly fee basis, but that was all. From there on, I was on my own. I'd have to hunt and scratch and dig just like he had to do when he was getting started. So much for goodwill.

I looked at Freema to throw me a rope, but she didn't. Faircloth's arrival, as well as his announcement, had all the earmarks of having been orchestrated.

That night, the moon was still full. I lay there in the hundred year-old spool bed Mom had been born in. Marshall and Frank had shared it as children, after which I had used it, and then it became Marshall's again.

As I tried to go to sleep, the house seemed to come alive. I had grown up in that house, but I never remembered hearing so many strange noises. At one point, I awoke with a start, sure that someone was standing over me. Was it Mom? It wouldn't be the last time I had such a sensation.

While I attempted to sleep, across town, a much more ominous scene was being played out in the kitchen at Buckeye Manor. A figure all dressed in black was illuminated only by the pure white light of the full moon shining through a window. The individual set down a black valise, picked up a pair of yellow rubber gloves off the snack cart, and stretched them on as tightly as possible. Moving with stealth, the gloved hands carefully opened the refrigerator door and began removing loaves of fruitcake from the back of the pile, placing them one at a time in the bottom of the valise. After removing a half-dozen or so, the darkly clothed figure closed the refrigerator gently, and left the kitchen without ever having been detected.

Quickly and quietly, the shape moved through the halls of Buckeye Manor, past the happy Santa, past the Three Wise Men, past the manger with baby Jesus, finally entering the gardener's closet. After scanning the shelves, the yellow rubber-gloved hands stopped at a bag containing the *Insta-Death* poison used to poison the bunnies and other creatures not to Muffie's liking.

The hands removed a bedpan from the valise and poured a portion of the white-powdered poison into it, taking care to make the batch small enough so that it would not be missed. Placing the bag of poison back on the shelf, the figure all dressed in black turned off the light and closed the door without detection. Something very sinister was beginning to unfold at Buckeye Manor.

CHAPTER 7

The next morning I felt the effects of sleeping on a mattress that should have been consigned to the Dower County Landfill before I was born. It was the same bed Mom had been sleeping in prior to her death. Strangely enough, my hip hurt in exactly the same place hers had. I'd heard of sympathy pains, but this was ridiculous.

I paid a visit to the bank to get a cash advance for Marty before going up to the office. I was in luck. Tori was the only teller working and she was available!

She had her head down counting money when I arrived at her window. "Are you free?" I asked. Without raising her head, she replied, "I may be cheap, but I'm not free!"

She looked up at me and smiled with those warm, chocolate-brown eyes that could melt butter and we both laughed. "What can I do for you, Mr. Majors?" she asked playfully.

I pushed my credit card across the counter toward her. "I need to send some money to my agent in L.A."

"You have an agent?" Tori asked excitedly.

Marty might not be on the 'A' list, he probably wasn't even on the 'B' or 'C' list, but Tori didn't need to know that. "Yeah," I replied confidently. "He's trying to sell a project I created to one of the networks."

Tori seemed impressed. "How much do you need?" she asked.

"A couple of hundred should do," I replied. Tori left to get the advance ready.

While I was waiting for her to return, Jack Peacock and his wife, Lena, entered the lobby. Jack and I had been friends in high school. He had met Lena in college and they now lived in Michigan. Lena made up about two of her husband.

In the course of our conversation, I learned that Jack's mother, Valoy Peacock, had quit teaching school following cancer surgery. She was now selling real estate to help pay her medical bills.

"I kinda figured my mother would go before yours," Jack observed with his usual dry wit.

"That's a terrible way to put it," Lena said as she slapped her husband on the arm. I told Jack and Lena I would give Jack's mother a call sometime and they left.

Momentarily, Tori returned with my cash advance. I signed the paperwork and she handed my card back to me. "I met your Great Aunt Cora. I really liked her," I said.

"I heard all about it, and I got the impression the feeling was mutual," Tori replied. Cora's endorsement ... that couldn't hurt.

I hesitated for a moment and then we both started to ask a question at the same time. "Would you ... Oh, excuse me ... you first ... no, you ..." We both laughed.

"Would you like to have dinner sometime?" I finally managed to say.

"Are you asking me out on a date, Sam Majors?"

"I, I guess I am," I stammered.

"Then I accept," she said without hesitation. "When?"

"Well, uh ... how about tonight?" I asked as she smiled.

Whew. That had been a lot easier than I'd expected. Tori gave me her address and I told her I'd pick her up at seven. She suggested The LEAKY Valve.

"The what?" I asked, not believing I'd heard right.

"The LEAKY Valve," she repeated laughing.

"Sounds more like the name of something I might hear one of my clients complain about."

"You've been gone from Friendly too long. It's this great dumpy little bar in an old warehouse. But if you'd rather not go there ..." Tori said offering me an out.

"What do they serve?" I asked skeptically, not sure I wanted to hear the answer.

"Ribs," Tori answered with enthusiasm. "Good, but greasy. We like to call 'em sliders."

"Aren't you Jewish?" I asked tentatively, not wanting to offend.

"What if I am? You got a problem with that?" Tori asked half teasing and half serious.

"No," I smiled, "it's just that you're different than any of the Jewish women I knew in L.A. And, well, I didn't think you'd eat pork."

"Oh, is that all," Tori said laughingly through that wonderful smile of hers. "They serve beef ribs as well as pork."

"If you're game, I'm game," I said, and left the bank.

I caught the elevator door just as it was closing and told the man standing by the buttons I was going to the third floor. "Sam Majors?" he asked as he extended his hand. "I'm Mark Tuttle."

"It's nice to meet you," I responded, as we shook hands.

"I'm glad you decided to come back," Mark said. "Your mother was a great help to me when I was trying to get started. If there's ever anything I can do to help you ..."

"Thanks. Thanks a lot," I said, grateful for this first bit of professional kindness shown me since my return home.

"Mind a friendly piece of advice?" Mark inquired.

It beats a piece of Friendly's judgment, I thought to myself. "Sure," I responded.

"Be careful whom you trust. It used to be you could rely on the word of any attorney in Friendly, but not anymore. Now I get everything in writing, and sometimes even that's not enough!"

The elevator door opened and we stepped out into the hall. "My mother always taught me that a man's word was his bond."

"Times have changed," Mark warned. "If somebody thinks they can get a client away from you, they won't think twice about stabbing you in the back." As we went to our respective offices, I thanked Mark for his advice.

Again, it was well after 10 a.m. when I finally arrived at the office. Freema hung up the phone when she saw me. She seemed frantic. "Where have you been? I've been trying to reach you for over an hour."

"I stopped to have coffee and read the morning paper," I responded defensively. "What's wrong now?"

"A nurse at the hospital called the office an hour ago. One of your mother's clients fell and broke her arm. She needs to know what to do with her," Freema explained.

"Did she know Mom passed away?" I asked.

"Yes," Freema replied, "but the doctor had seen the ad your brother placed in the paper, so he had her call anyway. She sounded pretty desperate."

"What did you tell her to do?" I asked.

"I didn't tell her anything. I don't have any authority. Your mother was her Power of Attorney," Freema said.

"What's the client's name?" I asked.

"Gretta Von Heimlich."

"Gretta Von Heimlich?" I laughed. "You've got to be kidding."

"I never joke about our clients," Freema responded without emotion. "She lives out in the country on one of the six farms her husband left her."

"Doesn't she have any children to take care of her?" I asked.

"No, she never had any children. That's why she appointed your mother her Power of Attorney." I was learning that many of my mother's elderly clients had no one else to care for them.

"Well, what am I supposed to do?" I asked.

"You'd better go out to the hospital and see her. I've prepared a document naming you as her new Power of Attorney in case she wants to sign it," Freema explained as she pulled the document out of her typewriter.

Mom's idea of automation was the lone electric typewriter Freema used. She had resisted the age of computers that were just beginning to take hold in 1989. It had been a major breakthrough several years before her death when Mom had finally acquired her own table-top copying machine.

Freema laid the paper in front of me and gave me a ten-second primer. "She'll have to sign it here, and it'll have to be witnessed and notarized here and here," Freema said pointing to the proper places. "Be sure to ask her in front of the witnesses and the notary if she is signing as her voluntary act and deed."

Freema placed the document in a briefcase and handed it to me. "Oh, and one more thing," she cautioned. Gretta is from Germany and doesn't speak very good English, so you'll have to speak slowly."

I turned to Freema and thanked her as I opened the door to leave. She heaved a nervous sigh of exhaustion as she wished me good luck.

I drove Mom's car into the parking lot of Friendly's only community hospital, the Dower County Regional Care Center, or "D and C," as the locals liked to call it. I hurried through the emergency room door and stopped to inquire of a nurse making up a gurney as to where I could find Mrs. Von Heimlich.

"You're Margaret Majors' son, the attorney?" she asked hopefully.

"Yes ma'am, I am," I said.

"Oh, good. She's right back there," the nurse said pointing to the back of the room that was obscured by a large white curtain that had been drawn for privacy. "When she told us your mother was her attorney, I didn't have the heart to tell her she had passed away."

I approached the curtain slowly, took a deep breath, and then peered around with caution. Gretta Von Heimlich was a wiry old woman with deep-set sunken eyes. She was clothed in a worn plaid bathrobe. Braided hair hung down her back. I judged her to be in her late eighties. She was sitting on a gurney, staring vacantly off into space. The hospital had placed her arm in a sling.

Seated next to her was a stocky old man, whom I would later learn was her married boyfriend, Harold Hardesty. He was wearing tattered dirty overhauls and was holding Gretta's good hand.

"Cheer up, Mama," Harold said. "You want me to get in your knickers?" he teased. "I know how much you like my wiener schnitzel."

"Not today, mein strudel," Gretta answered in her broken German accent. "Mein arm pains me too much."

Nothing I had encountered in Hollywood could have prepared me for this. I tried to keep my composure as I cleared my throat to announce my presence. Only Harold looked up when I came around the curtain.

I bent down to Gretta's level. "Mrs. Von Heimlich? I'm Sam Majors. Do you remember my mother, Margaret Majors?"

"Ja," Gretta replied. "She ist ein veddy nice laty, ein goot advocat. But plis, call me Gretta."

Placing my hand on her good arm I said, "I'm sorry to have to tell you this, but she passed away last week."

"I am veddy soory to hear dat. I am sure you are veddy sad," Gretta said.

"It has been hard, Gretta," I replied. "But the good news is I am also an attorney, and am going to be continuing her law practice."

"Dat ist nice," Gretta replied.

"The hospital called this morning because they needed to know what to do, so I came out to help. Can you tell me what happened?" I asked. Gretta grew very animated.

"Vell, I vas standink by my kitchen vindow, vatching da birds, vhen I hert ein noize behint me. I turnt arount and dere vas ein ugly old vitch pointink her broom and laughink at me—just like thee vun in Hansel und Gretel. I tolt her to get out of mein house! But nein, she vouldn't leaf. Den she vaved her arms und cast a spell uber me vich mate me veddy, veddy dizzy. Und dat ist alles I remember."

California might be the land of fruits and nuts, but that beat the hell out of anything I'd ever heard or seen in L.A. I looked over at the elderly gentleman sitting next to her, who was obviously very saddened by the circumstances.

"I'm Harold Hardesty. I'm the one who found her." Harold's eyes filled with tears. "Why did this have to happen now, dammit? Why?"

Just then a doctor entered the room with the charge nurse. "Are you the attorney?" he asked.

"Yes sir, I'm Sam Majors," I replied. He took me aside. I could observe Harold straining to eavesdrop.

"I'm Dr. Conroy. I was on call when they brought her in. She has a slight fracture in her upper arm that will have to be in a sling. It should heal in several weeks, but she's going to require some nursing care."

"Do you think a nursing home would be best?" I asked.

"Under the circumstances, yes," the doctor replied.

"My mother was her Power of Attorney, but she is deceased." "Yes, I was sorry to hear of her passing," said the doctor. "I had a lot of respect for your mother."

I was beginning to realize that it's a lot easier to come back to a good name than to a bad one. "I have a new document naming me as her Power of Attorney," I continued. "Do you think she's competent to sign it?"

Freema hadn't versed me on that important question, but somehow I had known to ask it. Was this another case of Mom looking over my shoulder?

"Do you mean is she competent at this particular point in time?" the doctor asked as he studied Gretta. He thought for a moment and said, "Yes. She may have had a mild stroke, but she seems to know what is going on."

"Would you and your nurse be willing to sign as witnesses on the document?" I asked. "And does the hospital have someone who can notarize Gretta's signature? I can't do it because I am named as the attorney-in-fact."

"I believe that could be arranged," the doctor replied, relieved to have the situation resolved.

"Let me talk with her and see what she says," I said as I pulled the Power of Attorney from my briefcase. I bent down in front of Gretta again. "The doctor tells me you've broken your arm. It's going to take a few weeks to heal, and he thinks you'd do better with some nursing care."

Harold interrupted me with fear in his voice. "You're not going to put her in a nursing home?" As gently as possible, I tried to be reassuring. "The doctor thinks it would be best for now."

"But me and Gretty was gonna enter the Polkafest next week," Harold cried.

"I don't think she's going to be doing any dancing for a while," Dr. Conroy advised.

Harold began to whimper. "But not the nut house," he begged. "She'll never get well!"

"The nut house?" I asked, not sure I had heard him right.

The doctor leaned down and whispered in my ear, "That's how some of the locals refer to Buckeye Manor."

I thought it best not to respond to Harold's fears, so I opened the briefcase and pulled out the new Power of Attorney. "Gretta," I asked, "would you like me to become your Power of Attorney now?"

Gretta stared at me for a moment before deciding. I knew she was sizing me up. "You haf kind eyes, just like your mutter. Ja, I guess dat vud be goot."

"Very well, then," I said. "You'll need to sign this document making me your new Power of Attorney. Would you like Harold to read it first?" I asked.

"I ain't much for readin'," Harold responded. "If you say it's all legal and proper, then we'll just have to take your word for it."

After the document had been signed and notarized by a hospital secretary as Freema had instructed, I left to make arrangements for Gretta at Buckeye Manor.

Meanwhile, over at the nursing home, behind a locked door, a pair of yellow rubber-gloved hands removed a fruitcake from a valise, cut the fruitcake into slices, and arranged several pieces on a paper plate. Next, the figure poured a small portion of the white powdery *Insta-Death* poison taken from the Gardener's closet out of the bedpan and into a small handkerchief. The handkerchief was tucked into a pocket for future use. Discovery had to be avoided at all cost.

When I arrived at Buckeye Manor, I parked next to a side door and entered the nursing home. As I walked past the door marked "Gardener's Closet," I thought to myself, *This must be Ronnie Trask's hangout.*

Suddenly I heard something like a pan falling. Having met some of my mother's clients, I was concerned that one of the residents might have wandered in there and fallen. I tried the door and it was locked.

"Hello, anyone in there?" I called as I tried the door again. There was no response. I decided I'd mention it to Nurse Swackhammer when I saw her. It was then I realized I had left my briefcase in the car.

Having retrieved it, I again entered the nursing home through the same side door when, who should I run into, literally, but

Aaron Longworth. He was in such a hurry to leave, he didn't even see me. Aaron was carrying a big black valise like the kind I had seen my father carry books in when he was going to trial. When Aaron stumbled and dropped the big briefcase, I tried to help him pick it up. "Excuse me, Mr. Longworth, may I help you?" I asked.

Before he had seen whom he had run into, Aaron replied gruffly, "No, I can get it myself." After he picked himself up and recognized me, he said, "What you doin' out here? Pimpin' up the old ladies?"

Needless to say, I didn't have a comeback, so I just stepped aside as he bulldozed his way past me and out the door. I walked into the nursing home and up to the head nurse's station which was empty. Next to the nurse's station was an easel that read:

Avoid the Medicaid Trap
by
Pre-paying your Funeral Expenses
A special seminar with Maple Grove
Owner of the Maple Grove Funeral Home
and Maple Grove Cemetery

I sat down in one of the large over-stuffed chairs nearby and decided to wait. Heaven forbid I breach protocol at Checkpoint Charlie!

As I looked around, I realized that Muffie's 20-foot Christmas tree was gone, as were most of the other Christmas decorations that had been taken down and put away.

After several minutes I heard the squeak-squeak-squeak of the tea cart Audrey was pushing. It was laden with fruitcake. She, of course, was wearing her yellow rubber gloves. Momentarily, Willie arrived. He was wearing his gloves and in the process of locking his zipper.

"Where have you been, Willie?" Audrey demanded.

"Geez, can't a fellow even take a leak around here without gettin' yelled at?" Willie replied with indignation.

Audrey handed a piece of fruitcake to a resident sitting nearby.

Head Nurse Etta Swackhammer finally arrived, followed by Rush, Muffie's yappy little Shih Tzu. I approached the nurse's station with temerity as she removed a yellow glove from one of her hands. "Hi, Nurse Swackhammer!" I exclaimed, hoping to cash in on some of Freema's goodwill. Nurse Swackhammer glowered. She seemed so unfriendly that I wondered if she remembered meeting me. "Nurse Swackhammer, I'm Sam Majors, Margaret Majors' son. I was here the other day with Freema, remember?"

Nurse Swackhammer did not look up from the chart on which she was making notes. "Anyway," I continued, "I have an elderly client who broke her arm."

Nurse Swackhammer finally looked up, obviously annoyed by having to acknowledge me. "So," she said, "what does this have to do with the price of tea in China?"

I continued to try to be pleasant, even though my blood was beginning to boil at this woman's arrogance. "The doctor at the hospital said my client needs to be admitted to the nursing home. I am her Power of Attorney, and I need to know what arrangements have to be made to have her transferred here."

Nurse Swackhammer picked up the glove she had just laid down and began stretching it on as tightly as possible. "You'll have to speak with Mrs. Welsh. She does all the admitting. Her office is down the hall," Nurse Swackhammer said, as she pointed without making eye contact.

"Thank you," I replied, as I started to walk away. And then I remembered, "By the way, you might want to check the gardener's closet. On my way in, I heard something fall in there and was concerned it might be a resident." Having done my duty, I turned and walked away. I didn't need eyes in the back of my head to know that Nurse Swackhammer's beady little eyes were boring into my back just as they had done the day I was there with Freema.

Suddenly and without warning, Rush grabbed my left pant leg with his teeth. "Heel, Rush, heel!" Nurse Swackhammer commanded. The little dog trotted dutifully back to her side.

"What's wrong with him?" I asked.

"Animals always know," she replied. Her eyes had become little green slits, made all the more ominous by the halo of fiery red hair and eyebrows that crowned them.

Meanwhile, unbeknownst to me, down the hall inside the owner's office, Maple Grove was sitting across the desk from Muffie Welsh. Inside Muffie's office, Maple was telling one of his bad jokes. Muffie was sporting her latest reincarnation—the Marilyn Monroe platinum blonde look she had tried 35 years earlier as a cheerleader at Friendly High School.

"So she dumped her husband's ashes out on the table," Maple said, as he emptied an ashtray on to the desk and began talking sarcastically in a faux female voice to the pile of debris. "Well, Howard, you know that Cadillac I always wanted but you said we couldn't afford? I'm driving it! And you know that vacation you'd never take me on? I'm taking it! And you know that blow job you always wanted? Well, here it is!" whereupon Maple blew all the ashes off the table as Muffie convulsed with laughter.

Then with feigned sincerity, Maple said, "You know, Muffie, your new hair color is really an answer to prayer."

"Is it now?" Muffie replied as a wicked grin passed across her face.

"No, I'm serious," Maple confessed. "Just the other day I was praying, please Lord, send me a blonde. I'm tired of squeezing blackheads." At that, Maple erupted in one of his hyena-like gales of laughter.

"You're so disgusting. Come here," Muffie commanded as she stood up and leaned across the desk, curling her index finger for him to come closer.

Maple stopped laughing long enough to lean forward, upon which Muffie grabbed his tie and pulled him across the desk. She whispered in his ear, "I have a little secret." Muffie then took Maple's head in her hands and pulled his ear toward her mouth while at the same time pressing his head into her abundant cleavage.

Whispering softly, she said, "Maple syrup always was my favorite topping."

Maple's eyes popped wide as he stared down into her ample endowments. When he pulled his head back, Muffie licked her large red wet lips very slowly.

Maple began to climb over the desk as he grunted back, "Then you're in luck, baby, 'cause Maple's sap is risin' fast!"

Suddenly Muffie's husband, Jack Welsh, burst into the room, ramming Maple in the back with the door knob. Muffie and Maple attempted to regain their composure. Jack Welsh was totally clueless as to what was going on between his wife and the undertaker.

Jack Welsh and Maple Grove couldn't have been more different. Muffie might have married Maple, but Jack's family had the money. Jack Welsh was bean-pole thin, balding and bespectacled. He also had a prominent Adam's apple and a high pitched voice which cracked occasionally when he got too excited.

"I found this fella wandering out in the hall. Says he's looking for you," Jack informed his wife.

Muffie sighed as she muttered to herself, "Probably another one of those damn charity cases. All right, show him in."

I entered the office, "Hi. I'm Sam Majors. Margaret Majors was my mother."

Muffie extended her French manicured hand for me to shake. "Hello. I'm Muffie Welsh. And this is Maple Grove."

"We've already met," I said.

"Well of course you have, what was I thinking?" Muffie gushed as she motioned for me to sit down. "I was so sorry to learn of your mother's death. She looked after the affairs of so many of our residents."

"Thank you," I replied. "I'm only beginning to realize how many lives she touched."

"What may I do for you, Mr. Majors, or may I call you Sam?"

"I prefer Sam," I said. "I'm going to be continuing my mother's practice, at least for the time being, but I've got a problem. One of my mother's clients fell this morning and needs to be admitted to the nursing home."

Muffie put on a pair of ultra-conservative reading glasses and reviewed a stack of papers sitting on her desk. "I'm sorry, but it looks like we filled our last opening yesterday."

"Are you sure?" I asked. The doctor at the hospital says she may have had a stroke and needs nursing care."

Muffie hesitated momentarily and then asked, "Does she have any funds?"

"My secretary tells me she owns six farms," I replied hopefully.

Muffie and Maple exchanged glances. Without hesitation, she picked up a pair of yellow rubber gloves sitting on her desk, and stretched them on tight. "Hmmm … we might have a bed. Would you like to come with me and check?"

"Sure, anything," I replied. "I'm desperate."

Muffie held out a pair of yellow rubber gloves to me. "Like some? You never know what you're likely to come in contact with."

I felt like a damn fool putting those things on but didn't want to do anything off putting to offend this nursing home diva. "Walk with me?" Muffie implored with a diminutive flair. She began a brisk walk down the hall past a sign that read: *Neighborhood for the Memory Impaired.*

I pointed to the sign and asked, "What does that mean?"

"This is where we put the people with advanced Alzheimer's disease," Muffie replied.

"Alzheimer's?" I asked. I'd never heard the term before.

"People who have lost their memory," Muffie replied. "We used to call it hardening of the arteries."

"Why isn't Rachel McDowell here?"

This area is reserved for our more aggressive residents," Muffie explained. "Mrs. McDowell wouldn't hurt a fly."

After hearing that, I wasn't so sure I wanted to go any farther, but I kept walking.

"Now, I wouldn't do this for just anyone," Muffie continued, "but I held your mother in such high regard, naturally I'd want to help her son."

"Thank you," I replied, trying to keep up with her.

We arrived at a pair of locked steel doors that had been painted pink. Each had a small square window at eye level equipped with the old fire safety glass with chicken wire in between the panes.

The Alzheimer's wing featured an all-glass nurse's station surrounded by residents' rooms like the spokes of a wheel. In the open space were 40 or so elderly residents sitting in wheel chairs, at tables, or just milling around. Periodically, an alarm would go off which indicated one of the residents had opened a door. That noise was mingled with the intermittent paging of nursing home personnel on the overused intercom system, which seemed much more pronounced in this section. *If I wasn't crazy when they brought me in here*, I thought to myself, *it wouldn't take long before I was certifiable.*

While some residents rocked back and forth, others just gazed off into space. One lady in a wheelchair was caressing a child's baby doll in her arms that she cradled with tender loving care. When she saw us, she attempted to hide the doll in her dress.

We approached a room from which came a very shrill, impassioned woman's voice crying, "Help me! Help me!! Help me!!!" As we passed the door, she cried out again even louder and more desperate, "Help me! Help me!! Help me!!!" I wanted to go in and see what her problem was, but Muffie was walking very fast, and I didn't think it wise to get separated.

A little farther on, we passed a very sweet looking, toothless old woman who also was sitting in a wheelchair. She smiled at me, so I smiled back and nodded, trying to be pleasant. All of a sudden and without warning, she let out a blood curdling banshee-like scream while she reached for me with clenched fists. "Aiyeeeeee!" she cried, her eyes filled with fiendish glee. I jumped back, completely unnerved, as I ran to catch up with Muffie. "This is awful. Can't anything be done to help these people?" I asked Muffie in despair.

"My hands are tied," she shrugged. "They are Alzheimer's cases, after all, and the government won't let us sedate them anymore." Warehousing for the elderly; that's what this was.

Surely, I thought to myself, *there must be a better way*.

Finally, we stopped at an open doorway. Muffie asked me to wait outside while she checked with the nurse. Next to the doorway was an elderly man who had a "lap restraint" that secured him to the gerry chair in which he was sitting—a sort of a recliner on wheels. On his lap were several slices of partially eaten fruitcake. He seemed harmless enough, so I smiled and said hello, upon which he pulled the upper dentures out of his mouth and began licking gummed fruitcake off of them. I almost lost my cookies right then and there. The lack of hygiene was beginning to make me appreciate Muffie's offer of the gloves.

From my vantage point, I could see Muffie talking to a nurse wearing yellow rubber gloves who was trimming the long, dirty, curled hammertoe nails of an old woman lying in one of the beds. I had never really thought about it, but someone had to perform chores like these. This nurse must have been a saint.

The nail hit the stainless steel bowl with a resounding "plink" that resonated off the walls, as I tried to pretend I wasn't hearing it.

"I'm going to be putting another person in this room," Muffie advised the nurse as she looked up from her chores.

"But both of these beds are occupied, and there's barely enough room as it is," she replied in disbelief.

"I'll have Jack move another bed in today," Muffie responded unfazed.

"But I thought you said the State inspector was coming next week." the nurse asked.

"It's only temporary. Someone is bound to die by then and we'll have an opening where we can move her."

"But I don't think …" the nurse started to reply.

Muffie cut her off. "I don't pay you to think. Just do as I say."

I saw the nurse's shoulders slump as Muffie left the room. I turned away as Muffie approached so she wouldn't know I had heard her conversation.

"It'll be tight," Muffie said, "but we'll be able to accept your client."

"Thank you," I heard myself mutter.

"I'm glad to do it for you, Mr. Majors," Muffie said, as she lowered her voice, "but please, don't tell anyone about this or everyone will want me to make exceptions."

As I walked away I thought to myself, *Can I really do this to Gretta?* But what choice did I have? This was the only nursing home in town. Maybe Muffie knew something I didn't. Heartless as it sounded, perhaps someone would die soon and there would be an opening.

Little did I know.

As long as I was out at the nursing home, I thought I might as well take Freema's advice and pay a call on some of our clients. My first stop was Rachel McDowell. I wondered if she would still be waiting for her daughter to arrive.

I knocked at the door before entering. Rachel's two roommates were asleep on their beds. Rachel was lying on her bed staring up at the ceiling. Her hands were folded and she had an angelic smile on her face. I had reached down to pat her on the hand when suddenly I pulled back. Her hands and finger nails were covered with something brown and crusty.

I went to the hall and asked a nurse to come look at Rachel. "What's wrong with her hands?" I asked with concern. "I just saw her yesterday, and she was fine."

The nurse hesitated, not wanting to answer my question. "It's … fecal matter," she replied reluctantly.

"It's what?" I asked, unable to believe my ears.

"Fecal matter," the nurse replied again.

"Fecal matter? All dried and crusty on her hands? That's gross!" I exclaimed, completely repulsed.

"She likes to get her hands down in her pants and play with it," the nurse said apologetically. "We clean her up, but it doesn't do any good. I'll take care of it right away."

An axiom I'd heard Dad use when I was growing up began to make sense to me at that moment. "Once an adult and twice a child."

The nurse picked up a wet washcloth as I left the room shaking my head in disgust. *For whatever these residents were paying,* I thought to myself, *Muffie could do a better job of taking care of them.*

I walked down to Opal Thomas' room and was just about to knock on her door when I saw the man whose photo I recognized from the billboard, Revered Freelander, bend down by her good ear. "Jest think, Opal," he shouted, "your sponsorship of the eternal flame a burnin' on top of our new steeple would shine like a beacon o' hope in the night …"

The Reverend grew increasingly dramatic. "Why, you could sit right here in your room every night a watchin' that flame a' flickuh knowin' your gift played an important part in guidin' the hopeless and lost to a haven o' safety."

Opal thought a moment. "But how could I see the flame?" she asked. "I'm blind."

"Good for Opal," I chuckled to myself. "She's nobody's fool."

"Oh ..." said Reverend Freelander, temporarily caught off guard. "Well I was talkin' about your spiritual sight, of course. Or, if you'd like, you could remember the church in your Last Will and Testament. That way you'd go to heaven a knowin' you left somethin' for the Glory O' God."

This guy was really beginning to bug me.

"I've always tried to do what the Lord wanted," Opal shouted.

"I'm sure you have, Opal, I'm sure you have," replied the Reverend. "You don't have to make any decisions now. Why don't you pray about it and ask God what He wants you to do."

All right," said Opal. "I will."

"Praise the Lord, Sister," Reverend Freelander shouted as he stood up to leave. "I'll be out to see you again real soon."

I stepped away from the doorway to avoid detection. I decided this might not be the best time to see Opal, so I would visit Cora instead. At least she seemed normal.

Cora's door was ajar, so I stuck my head in. "Anyone home?" I called out. Cora was kneeling to my right in front of the open refrigerator. She stood up when she heard me and closed the door. "Sam, you startled me!" she exclaimed.

"I'm sorry, Cora, I just stopped by to say hi. Did you let that man out of your refrigerator yet?"

Cora turned around and looked at the refrigerator. "Huh? Oh, why, yes," she replied laughing. "I finally let him go."

When Cora turned, her handkerchief fell out of her pocket onto the floor. "You dropped your handkerchief," I said as I bent down to pick it up for her.

Before I could retrieve it, though, Cora had already bent down and scooped it up herself. I was amazed at the incredible energy of this almost 90-year-old woman.

"Cora, to what do you attribute your good health?" I asked.

She thought a moment and then replied definitively, "clean living."

I grinned as I leaned into her and lowered my voice. "You know, if you ever get sick, we're going to begin to wonder …"

A wry smile passed across Cora's lips as she chuckled. "Can you come in and sit down?"

"I really can't," I replied, grinning. "I have a date tonight."

"It wouldn't happen to be with a pretty young teller who works at the bank, would it?"

"Maybe," I said, my grin widening.

"Good for you," Cora said, smiling. "Come back when you can stay longer. Perhaps the three of us can have dinner sometime."

"I'd like that," I said.

On my way out, I noticed that the door to the Gardener's closet was ajar and the light was on. I stuck my head in and called out, "Anyone in there?" The room was empty. Nurse Swackhammer must have already checked it, I thought to myself.

The "Gardener's closet," as it was called, was located at the end of a hall and looked as though it had formerly been used as a resident's room. It had been subdivided into two sections separated by one of those hospital privacy curtains on a track. The curtain was open, and I couldn't help being just a little bit curious, so I entered the room.

There was a small cot that I assumed was where Ronnie slept.

There was an old beat up dresser and chair. Nearby were a T.V. and a V.C.R. that sat on a table next to a hot plate, and a lamp. A small apartment-sized refrigerator sat next to a small sink. It was very Spartan, but this was Ronnie's world.

The lone bit of decoration on the walls was a bulletin board that hung above Ronnie's bed. On it were pinned several newspaper clippings. Two of them were the obituaries of Ronnie's grandparents, who, the news articles indicated, had lived out their final days at Buckeye Manor. That explained how Muffie must have gotten her hands on Ronnie.

The other article was about the Special Olympics in which Ronnie had competed and won. His medal was pinned to the bulletin board next to the article that featured his picture. He looked so proud and happy. I felt ashamed for having been part of the group that must have made life hell for him in school.

It was surprising to me, then, to see that he had several of our class pictures from elementary and junior high school before he had been channeled off into special classes for slow learners.

In each of the pictures, I looked happy enough, and Ronnie appeared as I remembered him—wearing tattered clothes, having unkempt hair and looking like a deer caught in the headlights. He always appeared at the end of a row, several steps away from the other children who stood shoulder-to-shoulder. I resolved then and there that at the next opportunity, I was going to ask Ronnie to forgive me for the way I had treated him.

On the other side of the room, along the wall by the door where I had entered, stood some wooden shelves that held Ronnie's gardening supplies. My eyes were drawn to a box that featured a large skull and crossbones. I walked over, picked it up and read the label. "*Insta-Death* All Purpose Poison For Home & Garden." *This must be what Muffie asked Ronnie to use to kill the bunnies,* I thought to myself.

Suddenly I felt the presence of another person breathing down my neck. I turned my head just enough to see it was Ronnie looking over my shoulder. I was so startled, I dropped the box of poison and in the process knocked a watering can and several other items off the shelf.

I bent down and scooped the items up in my arms. "Ronnie, you scared the shit out of me!"

Ronnie grinned. "You going to kill some rabbits?"

"No, no," I stammered self-consciously. "I, I heard a noise in here earlier, and ... well ... I, I just wanted to make sure everything was okay."

After I placed the poison and the other items back on the shelf, there was a long moment of awkward silence. Remembering the bulletin board hanging on the wall, I tried to make conversation. "I see you have several of our class pictures hanging on the wall." Ronnie didn't respond.

"I … I don't know if you remember me, but I'm Sam Majors. We were in several classes together. My picture's up there, too," I said awkwardly as I pointed to myself in one of the photos.

Ronnie still didn't respond, but just continued to grin at me and breathe heavily through his nose.

"Look," I stammered, "I, I really want to apologize for the way I treated you in school. I, I know it probably hurt and I'm sorry … about teasing you and calling you names. Will you please forgive me?"

If Ronnie didn't respond soon, I didn't know what I was going to do next. He continued to grin at me for a moment and then he did the damndest thing. He took off that string of rabbit's feet which he wore so proudly around his neck and held one out to me. "Want one? They're for luck."

I was dumbfounded. Could this be for real? There was no malice, no recrimination, just the simplicity of Ronnie's gesture of kindness. I took Ronnie's gift and held it in my hands, like the treasure it was.

I looked him in the eyes and grinned back. "Thank you, Ronnie," I heard myself say. "I could use a little luck right now." And that was it—apology accepted.

I thanked him again and left the room. What a lesson in humility!

As I left the building and drove down the circular drive, my thoughts turned from Ronnie to Tori. I could hardly wait to get home and change so I could pick her up.

Back at the nursing home, a freshly bathed Rachel was still waiting for her daughter Eunice, so she was pleased when she saw she had a visitor. She smiled as she turned her head, "Why, hello," she said. "How nice to see you. Won't you come in?" It was snack time, and the visitor, who was wearing yellow rubber gloves, had several slices of fruitcake in hand on a plate. Rachel's caller moved around to the bedside table.

"For me?" Rachel asked with childlike innocent delight. After a brief moment of hesitation, Rachel's visitor turned away momentarily so as not to be observed. After dusting the fruitcake with *Insta-Death* poison, the visitor placed the fruitcake on the table close to Rachel so it would be within her easy reach.

"Thank you. Please come again," Rachel said, as the visitor nodded and then silently left the room, passing the lone Christmas decoration left in the hall—the happy Santa with that great big jolly grin on his face.

CHAPTER 8

The LEAKY Valve was all that its name implied, and more. I had been gone from Friendly too long. No one had ever opened anything like this in Friendly before. *But after living in Hollywood,* I thought to myself, *I should be game for anything*. The ribs were greasy but Tori was right—they were good.

The last bite slid down my throat as I sat there looking across the table at the most beautiful woman who had ever accepted one of my invitations to dinner. Away from work, she seemed even more attractive than she had in the bank. The flame from the candle danced in Tori's eyes as she laughed and smiled while I regaled her with some of my stories from Hollywood.

After a few glasses of wine, we began to loosen up and talk a little more about our inner feelings. Tori, I learned, had grown up in Miami, Florida. Her father was a commodities broker, her mother an interior designer. Both had roots in Friendly and had grown tired of the pressures of big city life. When her Great Aunt Cora had decided to leave the family farm and move to Buckeye Manor, Tori's parents decided to move back to Ohio and take up residence there. Tori's grandmother had been Cora's sister, and had married a Jewish man named Harvey Epstein. Their marriage was something that Cora's father had never been able to accept, being the good W.A.S.P. that he was. They had a son, Tori's father, who had moved the family to Miami in the early 1960's so he could more easily raise his children within his father's traditions, something he could not easily do in provincial little Friendly, Ohio.

I found out that Tori had been dating Neville for most of the two years she had been back in Friendly. He kept pushing for a more serious relationship that Tori said just never seemed to feel right. She said she had been considering taking the relationship to the next level, but was now having second thoughts. Was I to take that as a hopeful sign? I hoped so. Tori said family was very important to her. It seemed she was an old fashioned girl at heart. Just my type.

Now it was my turn and so I poured out my heart to Tori. I told her how bitter I was about recent events. Not only had I lost my mother, I had lost my dream as well. I had gone out to Hollywood to try and make a positive difference and what did I get for my trouble? My mother's death. I wanted to go back to California, but I just couldn't bear the thought of seeing everything my mother had worked so hard for evaporate into thin air. I told her I felt like a prison door had closed shut on me. Why, I asked Tori, had God done this to me?

The thing I will always remember most about that conversation was the look of compassion in her eyes. She understood I was still grieving.

Tori let me wallow in self-pity until I ran out of things to say. Then quietly, thoughtfully, she placed her hand on mine and told me what her Great-Aunt Cora always said, "Whenever God closes a door, He always opens a window." I stared at her for what seemed like a moment frozen in time. Had she been talking to my father?

The mood was suddenly broken when our waiter came over to the table with a cordless phone—still a relatively new device.

It was my younger half-brother, Clayton. Fortunately I'd told Freema where I was having dinner and he'd called her at home from the Dower County Hospital's emergency room.

Dad had been in a car accident. His injuries didn't appear life-threatening, Clayton said, but his head had bounced off the steering wheel when his car hit a tree and he was complaining of pain in his hip. *Damn*, I thought to myself, *why did this have to happen now?*

I offered to call a cab for Tori, but she would have none of that. She insisted on accompanying me to the hospital. Right then and there, I knew this one was a keeper.

We arrived at the hospital in record time. Clayton pounced on me as soon as we came through the door. The poor kid, I could tell he was scared. Dad was the only real constant in his young life.

He took me to our father who was lying on the same gurney in the very same room where I had talked to Gretta that morning. His head was bandaged, but he seemed to be fine—mostly embarrassed by his accident. By nature a very proud man, the accident couldn't have been my father's fault. Whose fault was it? Why, General Motors, of course! They had filled his car full of what he liked to call "Rockafeller tubes."

When I introduced Tori to my father, he immediately began pouring on the charm. He'd always been that way with women. Tori seemed to take it in stride; in fact, she even flirted back a little, which he loved.

The doctor on call asked if he could speak with me. Dad had already started to tell Tori some of his favorite war stories from his days as District Attorney. I knew he was good at least for 20 minutes, so I excused myself.

The doctor took me back to his office where he had the results from the scan of my father's head and the X-rays of his hip. It appeared a mini-stroke might have caused him to black out temporarily. The force of impact from hitting the tree had fractured his hip. The doctor advised that his hip could be pinned and he would walk again after some physical therapy. They would operate in the morning.

But there was something else that appeared much more ominous. My father's brain was shrinking. The doctor suggested it was probably the early onset of Alzheimer's disease. There was that word again. The doctor concluded by telling me that it probably wouldn't be long before Dad would start losing his short-term memory.

I was dumbfounded. In the course of one week, one parent dead and buried, the other with a disease the effects of which I was quickly learning were almost worse than death. It was just about more than I could bear. I wanted to bolt and run as fast as my legs would carry me.

I asked about the prognosis and the doctor said it could be years, months, or even shorter. Each case is different. In addition to the physiological effects, there are many other factors that play a role in the progression of the disease, such as environment, the outlook of the individual, and the quality of the family support structure. In the case of my father, about the only one he had to look after him was my 17-year-old half-brother. It didn't seem fair to place this kind of a burden on Clayton.

Dad would have to recuperate in a nursing home, at least temporarily. Based upon what I knew about Buckeye Manor, I could not in good conscience place him there, so I called Marshall. After I explained what had happened and my reservations about Buckeye Manor, we agreed we would have Dad transported to a nursing home in Cleveland close to Marshall, just as soon as he was able to ride in an ambulance.

I thanked the doctor and told him to make arrangements for the hip surgery, and that I would follow up with Dad's regular physician regarding the other problem. By the time I returned to the emergency room, my father was up to the climax of his professional life's story. Tori had been very attentive, which pleased him immensely. I was impressed by her patience and kindness.

After Dad was ensconced in a private room, I drove Tori home. For most of the ride, I didn't say a word. When we finally arrived at her apartment, Tori said, "Penny."

"Huh?" I asked, as I parked the car.

"Penny," she repeated, "for your thoughts."

"I'm sorry," I apologized.

"I'm afraid I got some bad news from the doctor, but I don't want to bore you with my problems," I said.

"Why don't you let me be the judge of that," Tori replied.

She seemed genuinely interested, so I decided to open up. "The doctor thinks my father may have something called Alzheimer's Disease."

"Alzheimer's Disease? I've never heard of it," Tori replied.

"Neither had I, but I'm sure learning fast. The doctor says it's a disease which robs the elderly of their ability to remember. Eventually, he won't even know me," I said, choking on my words.

"Oh, Sam, I'm so sorry," Tori said empathetically.

"Just when I thought things couldn't get any worse, now this. I don't know how much more I can take."

"Remember …" Tori started to say.

I interrupted her with sarcasm in my voice. "Life's a bitch and then you die?"

"That wasn't exactly what I had in mind," she said.

"I'm sorry, I shouldn't be so negative."

"You have every right," Tori responded. "I just wanted you to remember I'm here if you need me."

I gazed into Tori's eyes. So much understanding. Was this my soul mate? Without the hesitation or that awkward feeling that accompanies a first kiss, our lips met and we embraced. I'm not sure whether the tires ever touched the ground as I drove home that night.

CHAPTER 9

I was still basking in the glow of Friday night when I walked into the office Monday morning. "Good morning, Freema," I said as I breezed through the door.

As usual, I hadn't gotten there early enough. Freema was there waiting with a man I didn't recognize. "Good morning," she replied as she made a point of looking at her watch. "This is Mr. Dale. He's been anxious to talk to you."

"I'm sorry to have kept you waiting. I didn't know I had any appointments," I said as I shook his hand.

"I didn't have an appointment," he replied. "I just stopped in, hoping you could help."

I sat down next to Freema's desk and motioned for Mr. Dale to join me. "I'll be glad to help if I can. What's the problem?"

"Your mother drew a Power of Attorney from my Aunt Esther to me. Her doctor has said she isn't able to live alone anymore, so I moved her out to the nursing home this morning."

Interrupting Mr. Dale, I said, "But I just talked to Mrs. Welsh on Friday afternoon, and she said the nursing home was full."

"It is," said Mr. Dale shifting uncomfortably, "but Mrs. Welsh said she would make a special exception for my aunt. However, she made me promise I wouldn't tell, so I'd appreciate it if you would keep my confidence."

Without revealing that I had been asked to keep the same secret, I assured him that I would and inquired how I could be of help.

"I'm from out of town, and don't really know any realtors around here, so I wondered if you could suggest one I might use to sell Aunt Esther's house?"

"I think I know just the person," I replied. "Where is your aunt's house located?"

Mr. Dale handed me his card on which he had already written the address: 515 College Street. "The mother of a friend of mine is a realtor," I said. "I'll give her a call." Freema handed me the phone book as she excused herself.

Across town in her kitchen, Jack Peacock's mother, Valoy Peacock, was listening to the song, "Masquerade" from the musical, *Phantom of the Opera*, while she combed out her different colored wigs that were sitting on the kitchen table. She looked much older than her early fifties due to the radiation and chemotherapy treatments she had received. A lone wisp of hair was all that remained of her once elegant coiffure. In contrast to her circumstances, Valoy Peacock answered the phone perkily as she turned down the music in the background.

"Mrs. Peacock, this is Sam Majors."

"Hello, Sam, how are you? Say, I was awfully sorry to hear about your mother. She was a wonderful lady."

"Thank you, Mrs. Peacock," I said.

"Valoy, please call me Valoy," she insisted.

"Thank you. I'm going to be taking over my mother's law practice, and …"

"I know. I read that in the paper," Valoy interrupted again.

"Well, I ran into Jack the other day and he told me you're selling real estate now?" I questioned.

"That's right," Valoy replied.

"I have a gentleman in the office who needs to sell his aunt's house because she is now in the nursing home, and I was wondering whether you might be able to help us."

"Love to!" Valoy intoned with exuberance. "What's the address?"

At that point the second phone line began ringing. "Excuse me a moment, Valoy. I have to take another call." I put her on hold while I answered the other line. It was Muffie Welsh.

"She did?" I asked. "That's too bad. Did she suffer much?" Having returned to the office, Freema looked at me quizzically as I covered the mouthpiece to tell her that Rachel McDowell had passed away from heart failure in her sleep sometime Friday night. Maple had picked up Rachel's body pursuant to the wishes she had made known when she entered the nursing home.

I finished the conversation with Muffie by telling her that I'd take care of finalizing all the funeral arrangements with Maple.

I returned to Valoy who was still parked on the first line. We scheduled an appointment to meet with Mr. Dale at his aunt's house later that afternoon.

Later that day, I picked up some of Rachel's clothes at Buckeye Manor to take to Maple. As I approached the front steps to the funeral home, two somber, vulture-like old men dressed in black top coats, opened the front doors and beckoned for me to enter. Soft, ethereal funeral music floated through the air.

"Good afternoon, Mr. Majors. We've been expecting you," the first man said. If I'd had my eyes closed I would have sworn it was Boris Karloff. "May I take your coat?" he asked.

Without waiting for a reply, the second man took my coat by the shoulders and slipped it off. He disappeared in search of a closet.

"Is Mr. Grove in?" I asked. The man motioned toward a door at the end of a long dimly-lit hallway.

"Thank you," I said. As I walked the corridor, I passed several rooms on either side containing open caskets which were occupied. It was not until I got to the end of the hall that I could read the sign on the door that read *Embalming Room*. I was growing clammy. Was I supposed to go in there?

I pushed the door open. Immediately the smell hit me. Formaldehyde. I remembered it from Biology class when we dissected frogs. As my eyes began to water, I struggled to focus in the darkened room. A ceiling fan rotated slowly above a figure whose shadow was projected larger than life on the wall by the single lamp burning beside him as he bent over a table. From my perspective, it looked like Quasimodo.

"Mr., Mr. Grove?" I asked. The figure straightened up and froze, holding his yellow rubber glove-covered hands up as a doctor does after he has scrubbed for surgery. The lamp cast a long eerie shadow of the hands on the wall, broken only by the movement of the ceiling fan turning overhead.

It's ... It's Sam Majors. I brought some clothes for Rachel McDowell." Maple removed the gloves and flipped a switch illuminating the room with a buzzing fluorescent light. Both his nostrils were filled with large yellow nose plugs, I presumed because of the formaldehyde.

Maple stepped forward to shake my hand. "How nice to see you again! I just got Mr. Rinaldo here out of the cooler and was getting ready to put the finishing touches on his face," Maple said, as he gestured to a body under a white sheet lying on a gurney.

"I'm a little short-handed today," Maple continued as he pulled the sheet off—revealing the whole body. If that corpse hadn't been dressed, I know I would have bolted right then and there.

"Would you mind helping me lift him on to the slab?"

I stared at Maple in disbelief. Undaunted, Maple took Mr. Rinaldo by the shoulders and gestured for me to grab his shoes. I set my little grocery sack with Rachel's clothes down on the floor and complied with Maple's request in spite of myself.

The body landed with a resounding thud when we heaved it onto the slab.

Maple looked down at the corpse's mid-section, put two fingers on his lips, and laughed. "Oops! Looks like I forgot something."

Try as I might, I couldn't keep myself from looking at Mr. Rinaldo's crotch.

"Know what's dead and twelve inches long?" Maple asked with glee as my eyes nervously returned to his gaze. I shook my head, unable to answer.

The silence was broken as Maple zipped up Mr. Rinaldo's pants. "Nothin'," he replied in complete deadpan. "Nothin' … Get it? Nothin'!"

Maple let loose with one of his ear splitting hyena-like laughs that bounced off the concrete walls. I managed a faint smile and then walked over and picked up Rachel's clothes.

"Freema tells me that Rachel McDowell's daughter, Eunice, prearranged her mother's funeral with you several years ago."

"That's right," Maple replied. "We already have everything we need for the obituary and the service."

I informed Maple that because Rachel didn't have any family, I'd be applying to the court to serve as the Administrator of her estate. "Is her funeral paid for?" I asked.

"Oh, yes," he said. "Eunice selected the nicest funeral we offer. The money's in a trust account, though, so I don't get paid until we have had the viewing and the memorial service after which Rachel will be cremated." As an afterthought he added, "A shame about poor Eunice choking on that ham sandwich."

"Yes, it is. Well, here are some of Rachel's clothes," I said, handing him the sack. "Please call me when she is ready for the viewing."

"We aim to please," Maple replied as I started to leave.

When I reached the door, I could hear Maple talking to himself. "What's dead and twelve inches long. Nothin!" he said as he again erupted into hyena-like laughter. I rolled my eyes in disgust as I closed the door behind me.

CHAPTER 10

Several hours later, Mr. Dale and I walked up an old sidewalk heaved and broken by the roots from the large old maple trees growing in the front yard. His aunt's house was run down and badly in need of repair. I judged it to have been built sometime during the 1920's.

The inside was no better. The kitchen fixtures appeared original. A very old cast iron water heater that looked like an upended torpedo with rivets stood in the corner near the large double-bowl white porcelain sink. Oil cloth caked with years of cooking grease still hung on the kitchen walls. Ancient linoleum, cracked and worn from years of use, covered the floors. A single light bulb hung from the ceiling, suspended by an old frayed electrical cord.

"So how old is your aunt?" I asked Mr. Dale.

"92," he replied.

"Did she live here long?" I asked.

"My aunt and uncle set up housekeeping here right before the Depression. The house was a Sears Catalog home. It was a gift to them from my grandfather."

"You mean they actually ordered this through the Sears Catalog?" I asked.

"That's right," replied Mr. Dale. "It was delivered in pieces on the train."

This must have been the first pre-fab housing, I thought to myself.

We stopped in the front hall at the bottom of the steps. Mr. Dale pointed at a large brown spot in the middle of the bare wood floor. "This is really what made me know I had to do something.

"What is it?" I asked, not sure I really wanted to know.

"My aunt told me she hasn't been able to climb the stairs to use the bathroom for the last six months, so this is where she would squat over a bucket. I'm afraid her aim wasn't very good."

I looked at the brown spot on the floor. How sad, I thought to myself.

"I'd have done something sooner," he said, "but I had no idea how much my aunt had deteriorated. It wasn't until a neighbor called last week that I came down and discovered what was going on."

Needless to say, the room wasn't exactly sweet smelling. As Mr. Dale struggled to open a window he told me, "I hauled 25 dumpsters full of trash out of this house."

"Did you sell the rest of the household goods?" I asked.

"What rest? There wasn't anything left worth saving," Mr. Dale replied.

"So this house is her only asset?" I asked, wondering how he was going to pay Muffie.

"Uncle Jasper always told Aunt Esther he'd left money for her, but he died before any of us could ever find out what he meant."

That didn't bode well for poor Aunt Esther, whom I'm sure would end up down at the County Home after the money from the sale of her house ran out. The Dower County Home for the infirm had been built at the end of the nineteenth century. It made Buckeye Manor look like a palace and should have been condemned years ago.

There was a knock at the door followed by a perky "Yoo-Hoo! Anyone home?" It was Valoy Peacock.

Valoy opened the front door and let herself in. She looked like the Golden Girl of the realtor set. I introduced her to Mr. Dale and she handed each of us one of her business cards that read: "Peacock Realty. We'll do you proud." How clever.

"Mr. Majors told me your aunt is in a nursing home?" Valoy asked.

"That's right," replied Mr. Dale. "And I'd like to get her home sold as soon as possible."

"I understand," Valoy replied sympathetically. "Sooner or later it comes to all of us."

Valoy surveyed the room and then ran her finger along the dusty mantle. "Well, it certainly looks lived in. May I see the rest?"

"The kitchen needs a little updating," Mr. Dale said as he led us to the back of the house. Valoy didn't realize it, but from my vantage point, I could see her upper lip curl with disgust as we entered the kitchen.

"How old is this house?" Valoy asked in a tone that sounded like she expected the answer to be older than dirt.

It was built in the mid-1920's," Mr. Dale replied. "My aunt and uncle took up housekeeping here."

"Well," Valoy sighed, "it might make a decent rental, if somebody wanted to fix it up." I could see Valoy's hope of a nice commission evaporating into thin air.

Mr. Dale opened a door off the kitchen. He snapped on a light inside the door and led us down a set of concrete steps into a dark dank cavern of a basement that had whitewashed, quarried stone walls and a dirt floor. Cobwebs awaited as we made our way down the stairs.

Shelves that once probably housed bushels of Aunt Esther's home canned goods lined one wall. Overhead was a single light-bulb hanging from the ceiling along with several clotheslines. A large coal furnace long ago converted to gas sat in the corner. At the bottom of the steps sat a mammoth old chest freezer that was probably large enough to handle enough food for a lifetime.

"I haven't seen one of these in years," Valoy remarked as Mr. Dale struggled to open the massive lid. I held my breath waiting to see what hidden treasure might lie within. To my disappointment, there was nothing but mold.

"I don't know how they ever got it down here or how we're ever going to get it out," he lamented.

Without hesitation, Valoy responded confidently, "No problem. If you let me list the house, I'll take care of it."

"Wonderful!" Mr. Dale replied with relief as he let the freezer lid close with a slam. "Where do I sign?"

Valoy pulled a listing agreement out of her purse and laid it on the freezer. After Mr. Dale signed it and gave Valoy a key, he locked up the house and we all left. Valoy was quite the sight as she drove off in her peacock blue Lincoln Town Car with the white top and sidewalls.

When I returned to the office a little after 5 p.m., Freema was still at her post, dutifully typing away. Mom had always appreciated the fact that her secretary wasn't a clock watcher.

Freema liked to compare a will she had typed to a white shirt after it had been ironed; both were so neat and perfect. I will say this for Freema, she was accurate—an asset learned in the days when one error meant retyping an entire document.

The front office actually had two desks. Mom's personal office was in the back down a long hall. The last few years of Mom's life, she didn't even go back there—preferring to sit out front with Freema and hold court when clients came in. Files were piled a foot deep on the secretary's desk Mom used. But if Mom ever needed a client's file, she could always put her finger on it. Mom had always possessed that kind of uncanny ability that probably irked my father, who never approached a problem with intuition. He preferred to work from lists.

The last few years of her life, Mom was really into entering contests and playing games. Freema said that if Mom didn't want to talk to someone, she'd just ignore them and go right on filling out her entry forms. She especially liked one sweepstakes company that sent her unsolicited gifts—essentially worthless trinkets— because she so liked getting surprises in the mail. When I learned that, it made me sad. I never realized how lonely she was. If I had, I would have sent her gifts regularly, in addition to my weekly telephone calls from Los Angeles. It's easy to understand how lonely senior citizens can fall victim to scams.

"Mr. Dale all taken care of?" Freema asked as I sat down by her desk.

"Yeah, I think so," I replied.

"There were several phone calls," Freema advised as she reviewed her telephone message pad. "Raymond Marvel is coming in to pick up his files."

"Didn't you tell him I was continuing mom's practice?" I asked. "Yes, I told him," Freema replied, "but he wants Neville Longworth to represent him now."

"Oh," I replied, unable to mask my disappointment.

Although I'd never met Raymond, his parents had been friends of my mother for many years. Every time a client left for greener pastures, I felt like I was losing my mother, one piece at a time. I took their leaving not only as a rejection of me, but also as the loss of another small part of what had been my mother's life. I hadn't yet learned that a successful law practice is dynamic, not static, and that the coming and going of clients is part of the warp and woof of it all. For now though, it was too soon after my mother's death and I was still grieving.

Funny thing—grief. It can sneak up on you when you least expect it and can be set off by the seemingly most insignificant things. Without warning, a wave of sadness would sweep over me. Time is the greatest healer, although I still don't think a person ever really gets over the death of a loved one—they just move on.

As I sat there, still stinging from this newest little bit of bad news, the telephone began ringing.

"Margaret Majors' Office," Freema answered. After a brief moment, she turned on the speaker phone. I could hear what sounded like an aviary in the background, a cacophony of chirping birds.

Freema covered the mouthpiece with her hand. "It's Pauline Cooper, one of your mother's clients."

"Freema! Freema!! Are you there?" The woman sounded desperate.

Freema gushed into the handset, "Pauline, my dear, how are you?"

"Not so good, I'm afraid," Pauline replied. "I need to talk to you about my Will."

"Weren't you aware that Margaret passed away?" Freema asked. "Her youngest son, Sam, is going to be continuing her practice."

"Yes, I read that in the paper. You can bring him along too if you like."

I'm just one step above chopped liver, I thought to myself, as Freema looked at the calendar.

"Would tomorrow morning at 10:30 be all right?"

"I guess so, if you can't come right now," Pauline replied. In the background it sounded like a door had been opened and then slammed shut. Freema started to hang up the phone and then stopped to listen.

Pauline's voice suddenly grew very old and very tired. She was talking to someone. "Here, take the phone."

A very angry woman demanded, "Who you talkin' to?"

"The lawyer," Pauline replied meekly.

"Which one? I told you I'd take care of that!" the woman shot back. The sound of the birds grew louder as if agitated and a parrot squawked several times. Then the line went dead. Freema looked very troubled.

"Who was that?" I asked.

"Pauline Cooper," Freema replied. "She's 90 and lives alone out in the country."

"What was with all those birds?" I asked.

"She raises them for a living. Every time she thought she'd found somebody to take care of them after she was gone, she'd want your mother to change her Will. Then she'd have a falling out with them and want her to change it again."

How sad, I thought to myself, as Freema disappeared into the file room.

A few seconds later, Raymond Marvel burst in. "Is Freema in?" he demanded brusquely.

Determined not to appear as just another piece of the furniture, I extended my hand. "May I help you? I'm Sam Majors."

Raymond shook my hand reluctantly, almost self-consciously. "I'm Raymond Marvel. I'm here to pick up my files."

I continued trying to be upbeat. "It's nice to meet you, Mr. Marvel. I heard my mother speak about your parents many times."

Raymond remained unimpressed. Freema returned carrying his files. She greeted him warmly, while I stood there thinking he was a traitor.

"Hi, Ray! Here is your file. Would you please sign this card for our records?"

Marvel signed the card and handed it to Freema as she gave him his file.

"We're certainly sorry to be losing you as a client, Ray."

"Yeah, well … Neville and I have known each other for a long time," he replied uncomfortably.

"Come on, Ray," Freema said grabbing his arm, "I'll walk you down the hall."

Raymond was halfway out the door before I managed to blurt out, "If there's ever anything I can do to help you ..."

Raymond stopped in the doorway, turned, and surveyed the office. "Must be nice fallin' into somethin' like this. If you ask me, you never should have left Friendly in the first place!"

With that, he slammed the door, leaving me standing there feeling naked and exposed. I found it hard to fathom how anyone could be that unfeeling toward someone who had just buried his mother.

In all fairness, for every client like Raymond Marvel, there were 20 whose goodwill did not end with my mother's death. It was the mean ones, though, the ones who had been such "good" friends of my mother while she was alive, that really surprised and shocked me. I was getting a crash course in life, and people.

That night, after I pulled into the garage at home, I just sat there with the motor running. I was driving my mother's car, living in her house, doing her job. *I might as well be wearing her clothes,* I thought to myself. I was deeply depressed. I have to admit it sounded very appealing to just go to sleep and not wake up.

Suicide? Checking out? Biting the big one? I thought about it. I suspect many who are overwhelmed with grief or depression consider it at some point—a permanent solution to a temporary problem. Like most though, I felt an internal check that prevented it from becoming any more than a passing thought. I also was afraid that what waited for me on the other side might be worse than the hell I was in already, although that was hard to imagine.

Whether I knew it or not, I was passing through a valley that would ultimately make me stronger. I'd need that strength for another test which lay ahead—one which would prove much more dark and ominous than anything I had encountered thus far.

CHAPTER 11

It had been several weeks since Mom's death, and much of the snow on the ground had melted. As I walked into the house from the garage, the telephone was ringing. It was Marshall calling to tell me that the results of Mom's biopsy had finally come back from the Mayo Clinic. The news was not good. The tests revealed she had contracted bone cancer that had metastasized.

Marshall reported that the doctor said he probably would have wanted to remove Mom's left leg, but that eventually she would have died a horribly painful death as the cancer spread throughout her body.

As hard as it was to lose my mother suddenly, it would have been much more painful to see her die a slow, agonizing death. That had always been one of her worst fears. Every time she came home from the nursing home after visiting her clients, she'd always say, "I hope I never have to lie there and suffer." It wouldn't have seemed fair for her life to end that way after she had spent it helping so many others. The news that she escaped such a fate made her death far easier to accept. God had granted her desire after all.

When Marshall told me the results of the autopsy, he swore me to secrecy. Whether it was his Victorian notion of death as evil, or the fact that Mom had contracted cancer, Marshall made it clear that no one must ever know the truth. In reality, most of those who had been close to our mother already suspected this to be the case.

When we finally got around to talking about how Dad was doing, I told Marshall, "He's been hinting about wanting to combine our practices. I don't know what I'm going to tell him when he comes home and starts asking again," I said.

Marshall cautioned, "If you agree, Freema will leave, and so will most of the clients."

"What am I supposed to do, then?" I wondered aloud.

"Just be patient. Time will take care of the problem," Marshall counseled.

I next told Marshall about how guilty Raymond Marvel made me feel for not being there to help Mom when she was alive.

"Mom didn't need you then, little brother, but she needs you now," was his reply.

There was a long silence on the line as I thought about what he had said. The big brother who had once been my chief tormentor had now become my comforter and champion. His words made it much easier to accept what fate had brought my way. The question remaining was whether I was going to be up to the challenge.

I thanked Marshall for being there for me. I hung up the phone, had a stiff drink, and went to bed.

Early the next morning, I awoke with a start from the bedside phone ringing in my ear. After a couple of fumbles, I managed to pick up the receiver. "He-Hello?" I answered, still half asleep.

"This Sam Majors?" an older man's voice asked. "This is Esther Dale's neighbor, Elder Johnson. Tom Dale told me you were taking care of his aunt's house?"

"That's right," I answered.

"You better get over here double quick, then. There's money all over the lawn and …"

I didn't wait for the rest of his words. I called the police ("Friendly's Finest," as locals liked to call them) and asked them to meet me there. I flew out the door, jumped in the car, and sped over to the Dale house.

When I arrived, I couldn't believe my eyes. The huge chest freezer was sticking halfway out of the back of the house. Two large, extremely coarse looking women and a skinny little man were picking up paper money scattered all over the yard which had fallen out of a hole in the house made by the freezer. With the help of the police and the neighbor, I was able to piece together what had happened.

After Valoy left us the day before, she had apparently driven past the Zeckman sisters, Bertha and Beulah Mae, who were down the street at another house loading some used furniture on to a beat-up old pick-up truck that bore a sign that read: *Ace Movers: We'll Move Anything*. Bertha's husband, Enos Zeckman, was standing nearby "supervising" when Valoy came upon the scene. Valoy learned that the two women were sisters, and that Beulah Mae had been married to him first.

After making arrangements to move the freezer, Valoy had given the trio a key and $20. She drove away, believing the matter would be taken care of. Enos wanted to move the freezer then, but because it was nearly time for "Phil Donahue," the sisters decided it could wait until the next morning.

The trio got an early start the next day because they didn't want to miss "Divorce Court" that came on at 10 a.m., right before the soaps. Elder Johnson had been drinking his morning coffee when he saw the motley crew pull up. He thought it strange that anyone would be moving at 7 a.m., but he thought it even stranger when he saw the man attach a long steel cable to the back of the truck and the two women disappear with the other end into the house through the back door.

Curiosity getting the best of him, Johnson came over to watch. Enos sat in the truck waiting for his cue. Johnson overheard Bertha shout impatiently, "Come on, lift your end up higher, dammit!"

Beulah Mae grunted back, "I'm trying!" They were in the basement so he couldn't see them.

After several futile attempts to get the freezer on to the stairs, Big Bertha bellowed, "Enos Zeckman, get your sorry ass down here and help us!"

Little Enos dutifully scrambled out of the truck and down the stairs. After several more tries, the three of them managed to get the freezer up several of the concrete steps.

Enos sprinted up the steps and back to the truck. Momentarily, Bertha bellowed up the stairs, again, "All right, give 'er the gas!"

Upon command, Enos gunned the engine. The truck lurched forward until the steel cable became taut.

The wheels spun for all their might as the freezer slowly inched up the concrete stairs aided by the gentle touch of the Zeckman sisters. Suddenly and without warning, the freezer seemed to take on a life of its own as it catapulted up the basement stairs until … WHAM … it hit the back door of the house.

Unfortunately, no one had thought to compare the width of the freezer to that of the door opening. Physics being what it is, the freezer only made it halfway through. The force of the impact tore the entire door frame off, along with much of the old clapboard siding, leaving a gaping opening in the back of the house.

While the freezer stopped, the truck did not. When the steel behemoth became wedged in the door, the cable broke and Enos and the truck kept going … and going … and going … right into the detached garage behind the house. The only semblance of the truck that remained visible through the wreckage of the garage was the hand painted sign on the tailgate: LIKE WHAT YOU SEE? CALL A-C-E M-O-V-E.

Fortunately, for his sake, Elder Johnson had gone back to the shelter of his own home before the accident occurred. After hearing the noise, he saw Bertha and Beulah Mae climb out of the house over the freezer. As they stood there surveying the damage, Enos emerged from the wreckage, dazed and confused.

The poor little man's current wife, accompanied by his first wife, descended upon him for wrecking the truck, without ever even stopping to inquire whether he had been injured.

Then a strange thing began happening. Enos noticed it first, followed by Bertha and then Beulah Mae. Money, oversized vintage paper money, was floating through the air. Upon closer examination, the walls which had been torn open were full of it. The three were still scrambling to collect as much as they could when the police and I arrived almost simultaneously.

So this was where Esther Dale's husband had hidden his fortune. All totaled, it came to a little over $450,000. Who would've ever guessed?

That poor little old unassuming woman, reduced to squatting over a bucket for relief, had nearly half a million dollars. Now she would never have to worry about how she was going to pay for her care.

I'd heard of stories like this: people who'd lost their money during the Great Depression, and never trusted banks again, but I never thought I'd see one up close.

Had it not been for Valoy's hiring of the bumbling Zeckmans, that house might have been sold and no one would ever have known. I was beginning to learn that for every cloud there is a silver lining, All you have to do is look for it.

Later that day, after I had recovered from my encounter with the Zeckman sisters, Freema and I drove out to see Pauline Cooper. She lived in an old trailer up a long dusty lane out in the country.

We walked up the steps of the worn wooden deck that served as her front porch and I pushed the small square door chime built into the front door. It made a dull, tinny ding-dong.

Pauline Cooper answered the door in an old blouse and double knit slacks. She was still wearing the yellow rubber gloves she had been using to clean the numerous bird cages that lined the walls of her living room.

Pauline was tall, thin, and wiry with big eyes magnified by Coke bottle glasses. Her hair was a stringy salt and pepper grey, and sorely in need of washing.

Freema gushed as we stepped in, "Why, hello, Pauline, my dear. How are you?"

I followed Freema into the trailer and shut the door behind me. Freema introduced me and I was just about to shake Pauline's hand when a parakeet landed on my shoulder.

"Oh, I'm sorry," Pauline said, "just shoo him away."

"That's all right," I replied nervously. "I like birds."

"Oh, are you a bird lover, too?" Pauline asked with delight.

"I just love the little critters," I responded as I kept my eye peeled for any more incoming visitors.

"Oh? Which is your favorite?" Pauline asked.

I shifted uncomfortably trying to think of something to say. I was cornered and Freema was enjoying it. "The yellow bellied sapsucker," I shot back. "That's it, the yellow bellied sapsucker."

"Yes, they are nice," Pauline said as she motioned for us to sit down at an old chrome dinette set in her cluttered little kitchen.

She gave me the seat of honor next to her large parrot sitting on a perch whom she introduced as Polyester. Pauline opened the door of her 1950's Kelvinator, took out a plate laden with "A Little Taste of Heaven," and set it down on the table.

"Would you like some?" she asked as she gave a piece to the parrot. "Polyester just loves it."

Ever on a diet, Freema decided to pass. Not wanting to be rude, I agreed to take a slice. No sooner had I lifted a piece from the plate, than that damn parakeet flew off my shoulder and defecated on it dead center.

By now, Pauline was so busy taking her Will out of its envelope, that neither she nor Freema saw me nearly lose a finger to the parrot when I fed it the piece of "freshly frosted" fruitcake. I was always a big believer in recycling.

"Your mother was such a good friend to me," Pauline lamented, shaking her head.

"We're all going to miss Margaret a lot," Freema replied. "But Sam, here, is going to be continuing her law practice."

I smiled at Pauline as she studied me critically for a few moments.

Freema opened the briefcase, removed Pauline's file, a yellow legal pad, and a pen. "Now, what was it you wanted to talk about?" Freema asked.

Pauline hesitated a moment. "I ... I want to make some changes in my Will."

"All right," Freema said as she opened the file to examine the office copy of Pauline's latest Will. "Now let's see. Last fall, when Margaret redid your Will, you decided to leave everything to the Overmeyers with the understanding that they would take care of your birds after you are gone."

Pauline waved her hand with an air of dismissal. "They're out now! I want them out! I can't trust them anymore."

"What happened?" Freema asked surprised.

"They were over here last week and I was showing them one of my best antique bird calls, made of solid ivory, imported from Africa. After they left, it came up missing, and I know Charlie Overmeyer is the one who took it!"

"Ohhh ..." Freema shook her head. "Are you sure? I don't think Charlie would do anything like that."

"Neither did I," Pauline replied, "but it had to be him. I didn't show it to anyone else. I asked him about it, but he denied it, of course."

"Could it have fallen behind the furniture?" I inquired.

"I'll help you look," I offered, trying to be helpful.

"You needn't bother," Pauline replied. "It's not here."

"I'm sorry you've had a falling out with the Overmeyers, Pauline, but you do still have your daughter, Ethylene," Freema reminded her.

"Hmpfff! Some daughter," Pauline responded disdainfully. "She never pays any attention to me, and she doesn't approve of my birds. Says they're dirty. Can you imagine?"

Suddenly and without warning, a very masculine, rough-acting woman who reminded me of the Zeckman sisters, burst into the trailer with her arms full of groceries. *Surely this couldn't be Pauline's daughter*, I thought to myself.

Although her face was obscured by the bags she was carrying, her husky voice was recognizable as the one we had heard in the background when Pauline had called the office the day before. She was dressed in jeans and a matching jacket. A pair of well-worn combat boots completed the ensemble.

"They were out of Spam," she said to no one in particular, "so I got Hamburger Helper instead."

"Fine," Pauline replied, "just put it on the counter."

"Whose car is that …?" Jane started to ask until she turned around. Her face fell when she saw us.

After she set the bags down, Pauline introduced us. "This is my friend, Jane O'Donnel. Jane, this is my attorney, Freema Glick."

Freema quickly corrected her. "I'm just the secretary." Jane's eyes darted back and forth suspiciously from Freema to the papers she was holding. Jane did not appear to be happy about what she perceived to be going on, but Freema was not the least bit intimidated.

"This is Sam Majors, Margaret Majors' youngest son," Freema continued. "He is taking over his mother's law practice."

I smiled and tried to be pleasant. "Hi," Jane said, as she acknowledged me begrudgingly. Freema looked at Pauline for direction.

"Jane, dear," Pauline asked, "could you excuse us please? I have some business I need to talk over with Freema and Mr. Majors." Jane's frown quickly changed to a scowl as she left the trailer in a huff.

No sooner had the front door slammed than Polyester came to life. "Jane's a bitch! Jane's a bitch," she squawked. I had to pretend to cough and clear my throat to keep from laughing out loud.

Pauline rapped the bottom of the parrot's perch with her cane. "Quiet Poly, we have guests."

"Yes, well," Freema continued, "Where were we?"

"You wanted to redo your Will?" Freema reminded her.

That's right," Pauline replied, "and I want to leave everything to Jane."

Polyester spoke up again. "Awwwk! Jane's a bitch! Jane's a bitch!! All she wants is my money. She'll steal everything I have!"

Red faced, Pauline rapped Polyester's perch again with her cane. "I don't know where she picks up such things," Pauline said shaking her head. "One more word out of you, missy, and I'll put your lights out!" Pauline threatened the bird eye-to-eye.

As Pauline turned to take her seat, the mischievous bird cried out again, "Awwwk! No, not that! Don't let her do it! I'll be good."

Polyester seemed to pause just long enough for effect until Pauline was seated, then she started in again, "Jane's a bitch! Jane's a bitch!"

Pauline jumped to her feet. "That does it, Polyester. Company or not, you asked for it!"

I looked over at Freema as I thought to myself, *Surely she's not going to actually punch out the bird?*

Not to worry. Pauline picked up a plastic cover near the perch and slipped it over the top. The parrot stuck its beak out under the edge of the cover and followed it the whole way down, crying, "Awwwk! Help! Help!! I've fallen and I can't get up! Help! Help!" Her voice faded away.

"I'm sorry," Pauline apologized, "She's awfully jealous."

Freema shifted uncomfortably in her chair. "Pauline, are you sure you want to leave that woman everything you have? How well do you know her?"

"Yes, I'm sure," Pauline replied. "She's been very good to me, and she's promised to take care of my birds after I am gone if I put my house in her name."

Yeah, if by taking care of them means cooking them for dinner, I thought to myself.

"You want to put your house in her name?" Freema asked with concern. "She could put you out and then where would you be? You could end up homeless."

Pauline shook her head with certainty. "Jane would never do that. Besides, she said it would be simpler that way. When I die, it would already be taken care of—something about avoiding probate."

Pauline looked at me. "What do you think?"

I didn't know what to say, so I decided to punt. "I, I think I agree with Freema. Besides, I think you ought to leave your daughter something. After all, she is your daughter."

Freema chimed in, "Sam is right. You're just inviting a Will contest if you cut her out altogether. Have you thought about who you'd want to be your Executor?"

"Would you do it?" she asked Freema.

"Not me," Freema replied emphatically. "I think you should have Sam. He could make sure your birds are well taken care of."

Pauline looked at me. "Would you be willing? They are very valuable, you know."

The two women stared at me for what seemed an eternity. "Why, uh, sure," I said. "I guess I could do that."

Pauline heaved a sigh of relief. "Then it's settled. I'm so relieved to have that taken care of."

"And while you're at it," Freema continued, "I think you should make Sam your Power of Attorney to handle your financial affairs in case you ever get sick."

"Whatever you think is best," Pauline replied compliantly. I looked over at Freema who was smiling. Right before my very eyes, she had managed to turn the situation around without the client ever knowing what had happened. Mom had taught her well.

Thirty minutes later we were back at the office. Freema was busily typing up Pauline's papers when the phone rang.

After listening briefly, Freema turned to me and explained, "It's Etta Swackhammer. Opal wants to talk with you. She says it's an emergency."

I rolled my eyes. *What isn't an emergency,* I thought to myself as Freema handed me the phone. I strained to remember which one this was. *Oh, yes, the little blind lady with the shrill voice.*

"Hello, Opal? It's Sam, Sam Majors."

"Hello? Sam is that you? Is that you Sam? Are you there?" Opal's high pitched voice could easily be heard even after I had pulled the receiver away from my ear. I shouted back, hoping she could hear me with her one good ear.

"I'm here, Opal. It's Sam. What's wrong?"

"Can you come out?" Opal shouted back. "I have to talk with you."

"What's wrong, Opal?" I asked.

"I can't tell you over the telephone, can you come out?" she whispered.

"All right, Opal, I'll come out." I knew there was no use arguing.

Opal's voice broke. "Oh, thank you, thank you. And hurry!"

"Well," I sighed as I hung up the phone, "here we go again." As I left for the nursing home, Freema seemed amused. I got the impression she was enjoying my education.

At the nursing home, a figure wearing yellow rubber gloves and carrying a paper sack, cautiously approached the tea cart. The hands pulled several slices of fruitcake already dusted with *Insta-Death* All-Purpose poison from the sack and placed them carefully on top of the others sitting on the cart.

Outside, as I walked up the sidewalk, I was horrified to see a couple of bunnies about to snack on the tender green trunks of Muffie's trees. "Shoo! Go on. Get out of here, if you know what's good for you," I said as I chased them away.

When I opened the giant leaded glass door to the nursing home, I collided with Reverend Freelander who hadn't seen me coming. He dropped his large leather Bible and loose notebook pages flew everywhere. As I bent down to help him pick them up, I thought to myself, *What is it with this nursing home? People always seem to be dying to get out of here.*

"Let me help you," I said.

"That's all right," Reverend Freelander replied all out of breath. "I can get it," he said as he hastily stuffed the pages back into his Bible. He stood up, pulled his vest down over his belly, pushed his pompadour back and then hurried away looking like a schoolboy caught with his hand in the cookie jar.

Just down the hall, Audrey was pushing the tea cart accompanied by Willie. "It just breaks my heart to see these old people suffer," she said.

"God, I'm tired," Willie sighed without hearing her. "I'm glad Opal is the last one. Let's hurry and get this over with."

Audrey stopped the cart next to Opal's room. "Willie, you shouldn't take the Lord's name in vain! What you ought to be doing is trying to find more ways to help alleviate the suffering of these dear old people."

Willie laughed wickedly as he picked a crumpled paper sack up off the floor. "I bet I could think of something to alleviate their suffering."

Willie picked up the platter with the fruitcake that the mysterious figure had poisoned and headed into Opal's room.

"Wait, Willie!" Audrey called. "You've forgotten Mrs. Dale."

"No," he shot back, "I'm taking this to Opal."

"No," countered Audrey, "We're going to take care of Mrs. Dale first!" Audrey replied emphatically.

Willie's eyes grew large as he shrugged his shoulders. "Whatever you say." He followed Audrey into Esther Dale's room. She was lying in her bed, crying. Around her neck hung a furry rabbit's foot on a chain.

In her best perky voice, Audrey announced, "We brought you some fruitcake, Mrs. Dale."

Through her sobs, Mrs. Dale pleaded, "Will you please call my nephew, please."

Willie walked around to the other side of her bed. Taunting her, he said, "No can do, Grandma. He's the one who put you here."

Audrey glared at Willie through narrowed eyes.

"Please, please," Mrs. Dale begged. "I'll do anything. I just want to go home."

"Oh, don't pay any attention to him," Audrey said as she tried to comfort the old woman.

Audrey then took the top two pieces of fruitcake off the plate and set them down on a napkin beside Mrs. Dale. "Here, maybe this will make you feel better."

Mrs. Dale grabbed Audrey's arm. "Will you call him?" she asked desperately.

Audrey patted her on the cheek. "I'll tell the nurse."

"If I can't go home," Mrs. Dale sobbed, "then I, I ... just want to die!" Mrs. Dale buried her head in her hands as Willie and Audrey left the room.

Out front, at Checkpoint Charlie, Etta was manning her post. "Hello, Nurse Swackhammer. "How are you today?" I asked, while preparing to punt in case Rush suddenly emerged out of nowhere.

"Busy," Etta replied with her usual charm.

"Could you please tell me which room Mrs. Dale is in?" I asked as I signed in.

"Room 305, across from Opal Thomas," Etta replied.

As I passed the lounge, I recognized the strains of the "Too Fat Polka." Inside, Harold and Gretta were dancing up a storm. They were quite the pair—she with her arm in a sling and he with that limp left over from a childhood case of polio. When they saw me standing at the doorway, Harold danced Gretta over to say hello. As he swung her around, I saw she was wearing a furry rabbit's foot on a chain around her neck.

"Howdy, Sam! Me and Gretty are still gonna try 'n enter the Polkafest. Isn't that right, Mama?" Harold said breathlessly.

"Dat's right, Mein Strudel," Gretta answered with a wide smile that was missing several teeth. It did my heart good to see them both so happy.

"You want to join us?" Harold asked.

"No thanks. Maybe another time," I answered.

"Come on, mama. Let's go another round." The two of them danced off together as I walked away whistling the "Too Fat Polka." As I walked down the hall toward the rooms of Esther Dale and Opal Thomas, I encountered Aaron Longworth coming from the opposite direction. He was wearing a very loud, very plaid, sport coat with wide lapels that probably dated from the 1970's. When he saw me, his teeth clenched and his jaw became set.

"Hello, Mr. Longworth," I said. "I like your taste in sport coats."

"All my taste is in my mouth," he shot back as he shuffled on.

I had hoped to stop in to say hello to Mrs. Dale, but she appeared to be sleeping so sweetly, with her arms folded neatly across her chest, that I decided not to disturb her. I was glad to see that she had made the adjustment to the nursing home so well.

Opal was seated in her wheelchair, talking to herself as she had been the first day I met her with Freema. *What a sad life*, I thought to myself, *to have such limited horizons.* Freema told me that at one time, Opal had worked as a telephone operator.

I bent down by her good ear and shouted. "Opal, it's Sam."

As she had done before, she reached out and grabbed my hands, pulled them to her mouth and began to kiss them repeatedly. "Oh, Sam, I knew you wouldn't let me down. Thank you for coming. Thank you. Thank you. Thank you. You're just like your dear mother."

"What did you want to talk to me about, Opal?" I asked. Even though she couldn't see, out of force of habit, Opal had turned her head to make sure no one was listening. She lowered her voice and pulled me close so no one else could hear. "There's been a terrible explosion!" she whispered with great agitation as she rubbed the now not-so-furry little rabbit's foot which she held between her bony fingers.

"A terrible explosion?" I shouted back in shock.

"Shhhh! Someone might hear. Listen. God spoke to me early this morning and He told me He had planned to take me home today, but there was a terrible explosion in heaven and I couldn't go yet because my mansion had been blown to bits."

"Oh, now Opal, that's just ridiculous!" I heard myself shout without thinking. I'm ashamed to admit it, but for a moment, I lost my patience with that poor old soul and she began to cry.

As I straightened up and tried to regain my composure, I thought to myself, *What would Mom have done in a situation like this?*

That's when my eyes locked on an old worn needlepoint sampler hanging above Opal's bed that read: "I will never leave you or forsake you."

And then it hit me. I'd heard my mother say it many times while I was growing up—like the night Dad left her with three boys to raise and educate, a mortgage to pay, and no job with which to do it.

"I put my hand in His," she told me, and prayed, "I can't do this alone, Lord, but if you'll help me, we'll do it together." During all her trials, she had always believed God was by her side.

I bent down again by Opal's good ear and began shouting at the top my lungs. "God still loves you, Opal. He hasn't forgotten you. He would never leave you or forsake you. There hasn't been an explosion in heaven!"

I looked up at the doorway and saw two elderly women standing there, open-mouthed, staring at me as if I'd lost my mind. At that particular moment, I'd have been inclined to agree with them. When they realized I'd seen them, they looked at each other, muttered something unintelligible, and shuffled off.

Opal became insistent. "But it's true. That's why you've got to help me!"

I sighed as I dropped my head in surrender. "All right, Opal, what is it you want me to do?"

"I have to rewrite my Will," she replied. "What changes do you want to make?" I asked.

"I want to leave everything to that nice minister who's building that new church next door."

"Reverend Freelander? You want to give it all to him?" I asked incredulously.

"That's right," Opal nodded.

"But why?" I asked.

"God told me if I did, I'd have a new home in heaven."

"Well, have you prayed about it?" I asked Opal, searching for a way out.

"Oh, yes," she said, "and that's what I'm to do. And then she added, "I'm not getting any younger, you know."

I thought I'd better go along with her for now, at least until I'd talked with Freema. I told her not to worry—I'd take care of it. It wasn't easy, but I managed to finally wrestle free from her iron-like grip as she kissed my hands repeatedly.

As I left Opal's room, I encountered someone in a wheelchair whom I hadn't seen in years—Reverend John Wooley— a wise and wonderful man who had been the pastor of the church we attended as a family when I was young.

After we exchanged greetings and reminisced, I mentioned Reverend Freelander and told him I was troubled by some of the minister's methods.

Reverend Wooley smiled knowingly and asked, "Sam, have you ever been hungry?" I looked at him quizzically.

"Well," he continued, "Virgil has. He was one of twelve children. Anything he has, he's had to get on his own. He never attended school beyond the eighth grade, and hasn't had all of the advantages that you and I have had."

"But he's so brash and overbearing," I countered.

"I suspect the same may have been said about that rough old fisherman who became Peter the Apostle. God has a way of knocking off our rough edges. There are a lot of people who attend Virgil's church, who would never darken the door of a more conventional congregation. Remember, son, we're all playing for the same team."

"Are we?" I asked.

"Well if we aren't, the situation will take care of itself. The Truth will always out."

I thanked my friend for his wise counsel and walked away. As I rounded a corner, I was shocked to see Mrs. Dale lying on a gurney in the hall. Maple Grove was just about to cover her face with a sheet. Muffie and Etta were standing nearby, along with a man I'd never seen before. He was a tall, gaunt, creepy looking character with large haunting eyes in sunken sockets, huge bushy eyebrows, gray hair and flicks of white foam around the edges of his mouth. His voice was low and gravelly and his oversized ears protruded prominently from the sides of his head. All four individuals were wearing yellow rubber gloves.

"What happened to Mrs. Dale?" I asked.

"Heart failure," Maple replied matter of factly, as he cinched a belt tightly across her feet.

"But I just looked in on her when I got here," I said. "She was fine. Did anyone call a doctor?"

Nurse Swackhammer glared at me. "Dr. Thanatopsies was here making his rounds, but it was too late!"

"This is Dr. Thanatopsies," Muffie spoke up. "He's our resident nursing home physician."

Dr. Thanatopsies? That name sounded familiar.

"Dr. Thanatopsies, aren't you also the Dower County Coroner?" I inquired.

"One and the same," he responded in a gravelly monotone.

"I'm Sam Majors. Margaret Majors was my mother. I'm taking over her practice. Mrs. Dale was one of my clients."

Dr. Thanatopsies removed one of his gloves to shake my hand. "I'm glad Mrs. Dale didn't have to ... suffer much," he said, hesitating for emphasis. With impeccable timing, one of Mrs. Dale's hands slipped off the gurney. Maple hurriedly shoved it back up under the sheet.

I shook my head in disbelief. "I just don't understand it. When I got here, she seemed to be sleeping so peacefully."

"Well, she was 92, after all," Muffie rationalized. "And she was very unhappy about having to leave her home. She told me that when I admitted her."

"It's probably ... better this way," Dr. Thanatopsies said, hesitating again for emphasis. Something about his delivery made me uncomfortable. It was too calculated.

As I watched Maple prepare to round a corner with the gurney carrying Mrs. Dale's body, her hand fell down from under the sheet again. This time Maple paid no attention as he wheeled her down the hall. It was a very unsettling sight.

I decided what I needed was a sugar fix. Since I had to pass the nursing home's ice cream parlor on my way out, I thought I might as well stop and get something to eat. I was about to enter but stopped short when I heard my name mentioned. Peering around the corner of the door, I saw the backs of Cora and Tori. It was late in the day and Tori was at the nursing home visiting her great aunt.

"I like Sam Majors a lot better than that other fella' you been goin' with," Cora said. "Better to pick a barrel of apples that'll keep through the winter, that's what my grandmother always used to tell me." I laughed to myself. *I'd been compared to a lot of things in my life, but never to a barrel of apples.*

"What's that supposed to mean, Aunt Cora?" Tori asked between bites of ice cream.

"When you choose your mate, pick one that'll weather the hard times as well as the good ones."

Boy, oh, boy, I thought to myself. *Cora doesn't waste any time.*

"I like Sam," Tori said, "a lot, but he seems kind of unsettled."

Cora looked up from her ice cream and turned her head and winked at Tori. "Sometimes fruit is sweeter if you give it time to ripen."

I smiled to myself, and decided to return to the office. *This was a better sugar fix than any ice cream.*

CHAPTER 12

That evening, I returned to Buckeye Manor at Cora's request. Having cleared Checkpoint Charlie, I passed the chapel where the good Reverend was preaching to a group in wheelchairs. "As the Good Book says, Brothers and Sisters, give and it shall be given unto you. Good measure, pressed down, shaken together and running over! The Lord loves a cheerful giver …"

As I continued down the hall, I could hear polka music coming from the lounge. The song was "Roll Out the Barrel, We'll Have a Barrel of Fun." *Harold and Gretta must be at it again,* I thought to myself.

The music stopped abruptly as a needle scraped across the vinyl record. Suddenly Harold came charging out of the room. He had a big grin on his face, a twinkle in his eye, and a spring in his limp.

"Hi, Sammy, boy!" Harold shouted as he pulled up his zipper. "I was just gettin' my daily dose of Vitamin P!"

I looked at him for a moment. "There's no such thing as ..."
Suddenly the light dawned. I laughed to myself as I watched Harold
limp merrily down the hall whistling a happy tune.

Cora's door was ajar when I arrived at her apartment. She was
seated at her baby grand piano playing "As Time Goes By" from
Casablanca.

"Recognize it?" Cora asked.

"It's one of my favorites," I said.

"Want me to play it again, Sam?" One of the things I loved
best about Cora was her sense of humor.

"I got to meet Bogie at a party once. He was the most
handsome man in Hollywood," Cora sighed.

I pointed to an oil portrait hanging above the piano. "Is that
you?" I asked.

"Yes, I had it painted just before I left California," Cora said
with a faraway look in her eye. "It's one of my most treasured
possessions."

"It's a shame you had to leave Hollywood. You might have
been big."

Cora rose to her feet, becoming the imperious Norma
Desmond from *Sunset Boulevard.* "I am big! It's the pictures that
got small."

I started clapping. "Very good! Gloria Swanson couldn't have
said it any better."

For a moment, Cora seemed lost in another time and place.

"Cora ... Cora ..." I prompted gently, "was there something
you wanted to see me about?" I was secretly hoping Tori might
arrive at any minute.

Cora crossed to the couch and sat down beside me. "I ... I'm
afraid I'm going to end up like a vegetable."

"A what?" I asked, thinking I hadn't heard her right.

"A vegetable. That's what Dr. Thanatopsies says could happen
if I have a stroke. He wants me to sign a Living Will. Do you
know what that is?"

I explained to Cora that a Living Will was a document used to indicate a person did not want to be kept alive by artificial means if they became terminally ill or permanently unconscious and couldn't make their wishes known.

I watched with curiosity as Cora reached down and groped around under the couch until she pulled out a large ashtray filled with cigarette butts and placed it on the coffee table. Next she removed a cigarette from a fancy cigarette case, and then stopped and looked at me. "Do you mind?" she asked politely.

"Be my guest," I replied.

Cora placed her cigarette in the cigarette holder she had removed from the ashtray, lit up using a vintage Zippo lighter, and exhaled a long plume of smoke.

"It's a pity Uncle Horace didn't have a Living Will."

"Uncle Horace?" I asked.

Cora took another drag. As the smoke slowly escaped from her mouth, she began to tell me the story.

"It was a hot and sultry summer day. I was only eight years old. My father and his brother, my Uncle Horace, were out working in the fields when somehow Uncle Horace got himself caught in the threshing machine. By the time father finally got him free, his body had been horribly mangled. They carried him into the parlor and sent for Doc Ruckman, but there was nothing that could be done. Uncle Horace lay there for two days, begging to die, until mercifully, he finally did. It was terrible. When it's my time, I hope I don't have to lie there and suffer." Cora took another drag on her cigarette and looked at me. "Do you think a Living Will is a good thing?"

I shifted uncomfortably in my seat. "Well, I'm not sure it's my place to say. Given the high cost of nursing care, and the progress that makes it possible to keep people alive longer, some claim it will lead to euthanasia for the elderly."

"Seems kind of funny," Cora chuckled, "if they're so worried about the mercy killing of old people, why do they call it euthanasia?" she asked, placing emphasis on the first syllable.

As another thick cloud of cigarette smoke settled over my head and shoulders, I tried to appear amused.

"I must confess," Cora said as she took another long drag on her cigarette, "there have been a lot of days I've wondered why I'm still here."

"If something happened where you couldn't communicate your wishes, would you want to be kept alive on a machine?" I asked.

"No! Absolutely not! Just let nature take its course."

"Well, then, that's your answer," I replied. "You are probably a good candidate for a Living Will."

"Thank you, Sam, for explaining that to me. You remind me so much of your mother. Now, let me see … there was something else I wanted to talk with you about. What was it?"

I leaned forward with anticipation. I could see it coming. Cora was going to give her blessing to a relationship with Tori. "Why can't I remember?" Cora lamented with frustration. "If I had another brain, it would be an orphan. You don't suppose I'm getting Old Timer's disease, do you?"

"You mean Alzheimer's?" I asked.

"Yes, that's it," Cora replied grinning.

"No," I replied reassuringly. "I don't think you've got it."

Cora looked at me and grinned. "I'll bet the nice thing about Alzheimer's is you get to meet so many new people every day." We both had a good laugh.

"Oh, yes, now I remember. I was wondering whether you would serve as the Executor of my estate."

"Me?" I asked with surprise.

"Why not? Your mother was my Executor and since she's gone now …" Cora hesitated momentarily. "You're not planning on going back to California, are you?"

"Well," I stammered, "not right away, anyway."

Cora looked at me maternally. "I know a certain pretty young lady and her ancient great aunt who'd be mighty sad if you did."

I smiled broadly.

"Wait right here. I have something to show you," Cora said as she got up from the couch and headed toward her bedroom. Halfway there, she stumbled and fell against a chair. I jumped to catch her. "Are you okay?" I asked with concern.

"Oh, yes. Sometimes I just get a little dizzy when I get up too fast. I must have forgotten to take my blood pressure medicine this morning. I'll be fine."

Cora broke away from me and disappeared into her bedroom. Suddenly the refrigerator started to thump and bang. It stopped when Cora reappeared carrying hangers with a half dozen garments on them.

"My funeral clothes."

"Your funeral clothes?" I exclaimed with eyes popping. This wasn't at all what I thought Cora had wanted to see me about. Sensing my discomfort, Cora observed, "After all, you never know when something unexpected might happen."

She laid the clothes down on a chair nearby and suggested I take notes. I dutifully pulled a pen and legal pad out of the briefcase I had brought along.

The first one she held up was a very garish red long flowing party dress with sequins and a big boa. The dress looked much longer than Cora was tall.

Holding up the bottom she said, "If I die at Christmas time, I want you to put this on me."

I gulped, at a loss for words. "It's … uh … it's kind of long, isn't it?"

Cora shrugged her shoulders. "Well, if it's cold, you can just wrap my feet in what's left over."

Cora laid that dress down and picked up the next. It was a double knit mumu with violent orange, yellow and purple flowers. Cora spread the 1970's frock across her body and whirled around like she was twenty. "If I die in the spring, put this on me with a lei around my neck and an orchid in my hair. I got it on my last trip to Hawaii. What do you think?"

"Uh, it's uh, colorful," I replied, completely at a loss for words.

Next, she picked up two other equally outrageous outfits. "If it's in the summer or the fall, either one of these will do."

My mouth must have been hanging open because Cora looked over at me and asked, "You writing this down?" I looked down at my legal pad. It was blank.

"Now if you don't like those, just use one of these." She held up two modestly elegant dresses.

I looked at Cora. She had a mischievous grin on her face and an ornery twinkle in her eye. I knew I had been had, and burst out laughing.

"You really had me going there."

"Well, a girl has to have a little fun," she told me.

While I had been visiting the elderly in the nursing home, unbeknownst to me at the time, Tori and Neville were across town having dinner at The Wagon Wheel Family Restaurant. He never would have been caught dead in a place like The LEAKY Valve. It might have hurt his precious image.

Neville was displaying his usual bravado. "You should have seen me. The poor guy didn't even have a chance. The jury found him guilty on all four counts. The judge said it was one of the best prosecutions he's seen in years."

"That's nice, Neville," Tori sighed, lost in thought.

"He also said I have a bright career ahead of me. You could wind up being married to a future judge!"

"That would be nice," Tori sighed again.

"You seem preoccupied, Baby. Something wrong with your Aunt Clara?" Neville asked as he shoveled in a bite of banana cream pie.

"Her name is Cora, and no, she's fine. I was just thinking how much courage it must have taken Sam Majors to come back here and take over his mother's law practice."

"Sam Majors!" Neville snapped. "What the hell has he got to do with anything?"

"Nothing," Tori answered regretfully, realizing what she had said. "I didn't mean to upset you."

"First I find you flirting with him in the bank, and now you're thinking about him when you're with me? Is there something going on between the two of you?"

"And what if there is?" Tori shot back angrily.

"Then I'd say you have a conflict of interest!" Neville answered curtly.

That night, I was at home making myself a sandwich when I accidentally dropped a jar of mayonnaise on the kitchen floor. When I opened the door to the broom closet to get something to use to pick up the shattered glass, it hit me: Mom's scent. Several of her old house coats were still hanging there and since the closet had been shut up since her death, they still smelled like Mom. I took one out, held it close to my face, and took a deep breath. For a moment, she was there again. Another unexpected wave of grief swept over me. After I put it back and cleaned up my mess, I closed the broom closet. I knew I would be back.

I settled down with my sandwich and a beer in front of the television to watch a video tape of *It's a Wonderful Life* on TV. The longer I watched, the more similarities I saw between George Bailey who felt trapped in Bedford Falls and myself who felt trapped in Friendly. It was very cathartic.

I had just gotten to the scene where there is a run on the Building and Loan and mean old Mr. Potter is threatening to close it down. George stands in what was his father's office looking at his father's picture on the wall. Beneath the picture hangs an obscure little plaque that caught my eye. I paused the tape so I could make out the words: "All you can take with you is that which you've given away." In the movie,

George Bailey ends up using his honeymoon money to save the Building and Loan by helping his friends and depositors in their time of need.

The little plaque is an obscure bit of set dressing, but it pretty much sums up the message of the movie, as well as my mother's life. She was rich because of the many selfless acts she'd done for others, a sharp contrast to the life of hot tubs, Perrier and BMW's that I'd imagined for myself in California.

I was startled out of my moment of contemplation when the telephone began ringing. It was the night nurse at Buckeye Manor. "I'm sorry to disturb you at this hour, but your home number was down to call in case of an emergency at night."

After Rachel's death, Freema had suggested I give my home telephone number to the nursing home in case anything happened to any of our clients when the office wasn't open.

"Are you Opal Thomas' next-of-kin?" she asked.

"We, we weren't related, but I guess I'm about all she had. What's wrong?" I asked.

The nurse hesitated momentarily. "Opal Thomas passed away this evening."

"Opal passed away?" Was that a lump in my throat? I was still not accustomed to receiving such news. I was beginning to relate to my mother's love for her clients who had become like family.

"Yes. Dr. Thanatopsies thinks it was probably heart failure. We wondered if you wanted us to call Maple Grove to have him pick up the body. Her chart says she is to be cremated."

"I guess so. If that's what she wanted." I hung up the receiver. *If this keeps up,* I thought to myself, *I'm not going to have any clients left.*

CHAPTER 13

When I walked into the office the next morning, Freema was busy reading the obituaries. "Well, nobody we know died."

"Isn't it in the paper?" I asked.

"Isn't what in the paper?"

"Opal's obituary. The nursing home called last night to tell me she'd passed away."

Freema grew stoic. "Awww. Poor Opal. She's probably better off. Is she down at the funeral home?"

Freema went to the safe to get Opal's Will as I scanned the paper. "Uh, huh. Well, if she had to go, I'm glad it happened before she could make out a new Will. I wonder who the good Reverend is going to get to pay for his new steeple now?"

Freema emerged from the file room reading Opal's Will. "Well, the Dower County Commissioners are going to be happy. Opal left everything she owned to the County to help pay for a new jail. Goodness knows, we need one."

"I don't believe it!" I exclaimed.

Freema looked up from the Will. "Her bequest may seem a little unorthodox, but Opal used to pass that old jail every day on the way to the phone company, and thought that was where her money could do the most good."

"Not that," I interrupted Freema. "Did you read the real estate transfers in the paper this morning? Listen to this: From Pauline Cooper to Jane O'Donnel, a part of the Northeast Quarter of the Southwest Quarter of Section Seventeen of Hero Township, Dower County, Ohio. Pauline gave her house to that awful woman!"

"Let me see that!" Freema exclaimed as she grabbed the paper. Freema's face fell. "Poor Pauline. Jane must have seen a copy of her new Will appointing you as the Executor. That explains it, then. While you were down in the bank yesterday, Jane O'Donnel stomped in here and demanded all of Pauline's files."

"You didn't give them to her, did you?" I asked incredulously.

"Of course not! I told her I'd have to talk with Pauline first."

Freema reached for the phone and dialed the County Recorder. "I'd like to check on a deed that was filed there yesterday. The Grantor was Pauline Cooper. Could you please tell me who prepared that instrument?" Freema's face fell as she listened.

"Well? Who was it?" I asked as Freema hung up the phone.

"Aaron Longworth," she replied grimly.

Later that morning, I found myself climbing the tall marble stairs to the ancient Dower County Courthouse. It was a grand old edifice which had been erected in the previous century by a master mason named Hiram Abiff.

I figured Mom had probably climbed those stairs a million times during her 50 years of practice and while she served as a judge. I pushed open the big heavy walnut door to the probate court where Mom had served as Judge when I was very young.

Inside, who should I encounter but Aaron Longworth, looking dapper as usual, regaling the probate clerks with some of his courtroom exploits. Attempting to hide my contempt, I said good morning and asked how he was doing.

"Up and dressed," Aaron shot back.

Judge Percy Corbin was standing nearby, so I extended my hand to Mr. Longworth in deference to a senior member of the bar. Aaron hobbled over to me, dragging one leg. He extended a shaky hand to me, rocked back on his heels, and made his eyelids flutter as if he was going to pass out. He put his hand up to his mouth so no one else could hear, even though he spoke loudly enough to make sure everyone did. "My syphilis is kickin' up on me."

I looked at two of the older clerks, both of whom Mom had hired when she was judge. They were shaking their heads and laughing to themselves at this child in a man's body. Aaron saw their expressions and loved it.

I approached the counter and pulled the file out from under my arm which contained the application to probate Opal Thomas' Last Will and Testament.

"Good morning, Judge."

"Good morning, Sam," the Judge replied.

Judge Corbin was very kind to me—another by-product of all the goodwill Mom had built up during her many years of practice. "I have a new estate."

"Another one?" one of the clerks exclaimed with surprise. As I set Opal's Will down on the counter, I could sense Aaron attempting to look over my shoulder at its contents.

"That's the third one this week, isn't it?" the Judge asked.

"Yes sir," I replied, as Aaron's jealous eyes burned holes through me.

"This one left all her money to the County Commissioners to help build a new jail. Three Hundred and Fifty Thousand Dollars."

Raising one eyebrow, Judge Corbin gazed at me intently. "It seems to me the fee on that size an estate ought to be in the neighborhood of Twenty-Five Thousand Dollars, Sam. I take it all these new estates mean you're going to be here for a long, long time?"

I swallowed hard. I seemed to be getting in deeper and deeper. "Uh, yes sir, I … I guess it does."

Aaron, who had miraculously recovered from his pseudo-syphilis attack, brushed brusquely past me.

"I'm glad you're feeling better, Mr. Longworth. By the way, I like your taste in sport coats," I called after him.

"Hmpfff!" Aaron grunted sarcastically. "All my taste is in my mouth."

Meanwhile, at Buckeye Manor, Lawrence Welk and his Champagne Music Makers were entertaining Gretta on television with a special edition of polka music. She had fallen asleep in her chair, next to her treasured autographed photo of Welk, which she kept right next to the picture of her boyfriend, Harold. Momentarily, someone wearing yellow rubber gloves entered her room carrying a plate of fruitcake. Observing that Gretta was asleep, they set the plate down next to her, taking careful pains to arrange the pieces ever so nicely.

After leaving the courthouse, I decided to pick up some authentic German strudel for Gretta because she was so fond of it. I stopped at a German bakery before going to the nursing home.

As I walked up the tree-lined sidewalk, I stopped dead in my tracks. There were a couple of bunnies lying next to one of Muffie's trees. Suddenly, Ronnie came running up from behind wearing a pair of yellow rubber gloves. Picking the bunnies up, he held his trophies by their lifeless little necks. "Look!" he guffawed loudly with glee. "More bunnies!" I nodded and hurried on into the nursing home.

When Nurse Swackhammer saw me approaching the front desk, the expression on her face could have scalded milk. *Maybe it would help,* I thought, *if she knew I was trying to follow in my mother's footsteps of caring for clients at the nursing home.*

I set the apple strudel down on the counter. "I brought some apple strudel for Gretta Von Heimlich. I thought it might cheer her up a bit," I said, hoping a little goodwill might rub off on Nurse Swackhammer as well.

But to no avail. Nurse Swackhammer didn't even bother to remove her yellow rubber gloves as she handed me the register which I signed and handed back to her.

As I approached Gretta's door, which was close to the nurse's station, I passed Willie pushing the squeaky tea cart laden with fruitcake. Momentarily, Audrey emerged from Gretta's room and rejoined Willie.

Gretta was watching Lawrence Welk conduct a polka when I knocked on her door and I asked if I could come in. Nurse Swackhammer's little friend, Rush, was sitting on her lap.

"Cume een! Cume een!" she exclaimed with her broken German accent and toothy grin.

Gretta clapped twice and the TV went black. "Rush unt I vere yust vatchink Mr. Velk. Ve tink he's wundebah. He efen zent me his photograph." Gretta pointed proudly to Lawrence Welk's photograph which he had autographed: "To Gretta, with love, Lawrence Welk."

"Do you efer vatch Mr. Velk on ze TV?" she asked.

"Oh, now and then," I lied, as I set the apple strudel down next to the fruitcake and removed the plastic wrap. I pulled my hand back quickly when Rush started to growl.

"Strudel! Dat iss nize of you," Gretta exclaimed with childlike delight.

"Looks like someone already beat me to the punch," I said, as I observed the fruitcake.

"Now, I vunder vere dat cume from? No matter. I luf alls kinds of strudel." Gretta looked at Harold's picture which was sitting next to Lawrence Welk's, and smiled a big toothy grin.

"I know. How is Harold, anyway?" I asked.

"He iz sehr geet." Gretta began to laugh. "Boot den, he iss alvayz geet," she exclaimed as she winked at me mischievously.

"And your arm?" I inquired.

"Ees better, danken. Doctor sayz I vill go home soon."

"That's nice," I replied with a smile.

"Vud you like to play mit Rush?" Gretta asked.

I looked at Rush who showed me his teeth again.

"No thanks, I have to go. I'll let you get back to Lawrence."

With a wave of her good arm, Gretta shouted "Auf Wiedersehen!" as I left the room.

Gretta clapped her hands again as she looked at the fruitcake and the strudel sitting on the table next to her. "Now vich shall ve eat first, Rush?"

My real purpose in coming to the nursing home had been to clean out Opal's room. Knowing Muffie, Opal's estate would be charged for every minute her things were still there.

Reluctantly, I made my way back to the front desk where I was told perfunctorily, "We needed to get the closet space ready for a new resident. You'll find Opal's things packed and waiting for you in a suitcase on her bed."

I thanked Nurse Swackhammer and turned to leave, when I couldn't keep up pretense any longer. I turned back toward her and observed, "You don't like me, do you?"

"I'm only paid to be nice to the residents," came the reply.

"Then I'd say you need a raise," I said, as I turned and began backing away. It was one of the rare moments in my life when I hadn't said too much or too little, but I'd made my point.

Nurse Swackhammer stopped writing, but didn't look up until I was gone.

I walked into Opal's room. Her bed was neatly made and a small worn suitcase was sitting on top of the bedspread. It made me sad to think that this was all that remained of a once active and vibrant life.

I gently opened the little suitcase. Inside on top was a small plaque from the Telephone Pioneers of America that Opal received when she retired in 1965. There was an old comb and a brush, a partially used cake of rouge, and an old tin of Cashmere Bouquet bath powder. I sifted through several items of worn clothing and there at the very bottom of the suitcase, I found Opal's most valued possession; a well-read, dog-eared *King James Bible*. I gently ran my fingers across the worn leather cover which was cracked from years of use before Opal had lost her sight. Inside were several old photographs I presumed to be of Opal's parents, her baptismal certificate and a letter yellowed with age. It was written in 1917 from a young man named Luther Searfoss who was serving in France during World War I. He told Opal of his undying love for her and promised to marry her when he returned from the war. When I turned the page, a fragile newspaper article fell out. It was his obituary. Shortly after he had written the letter, Luther had been killed on the front lines, and his body had remained in French soil. My heart grew heavy as I thought about the wonderful life Opal might have had with this man if his hadn't been cut short.

I looked up from the article and my gaze fixed upon Opal's old needlepoint sampler Muffie had overlooked in her zeal to ready the room for its next occupant. "I Will Never Leave You Or Forsake You." These are the words Opal must have clung to all those years when she felt alone. A smile came to my face as I realized she wasn't alone anymore.

The solemnity of the moment was broken by the intrusion of Reverend Freelander. "A shame about what happened to Sister Opal. God rest her soul. But she had her treasures stored up in heaven!"

I turned to look at him.

"I'm the Reverend Virgil Freelander. I was the one who offered Opal spiritual comfort in her last days."

"I know who you are, Reverend Freelander," I said as I turned back to the suitcase to hide those things which had been most sacred to Opal.

"I understand you're Opal's attorney, the one who'll be probatin' her estate?"

"That's right," I said as I closed the suitcase.

"Well," said the Reverend, "I saw you'd signed the guest register out front, so I thought I'd save you the trouble o' callin' me. You know, 'bout the bequest."

I looked at him quizzically, feigning surprise. "Bequest? What bequest?"

"The bequest in Sister Opal's Last Will and Testament—the one she left to help build the Renaissance New Faith Tabernacle."

"I know of no such bequest."

"What?" Reverend Freelander asked as his eyes began to grow large. "But I thought …"

"Opal never got her Will changed before she died," I said. "Everything she had—all $350,000—is going to the county to help build a new jail."

By now Reverend Freelander's face had turned beet red, his eyes were popping and his lower lip was shaking. Attempting to regain his composure, he pulled his vest down over his large stomach.

"I see. Well, I best be goin'. Always have to be about the Lord's work, you know." Reverend Freelander turned on his heel and left the room.

I was remembering my conversation with Reverend Wooley when Nurse Swackhammer appeared in the doorway pushing Pauline Cooper in a wheelchair. Muffie had wasted no time in reassigning Opal's room to Pauline, who was carrying a framed photograph of her pet parrot, Polyester, in her arms.

"Pauline!" I exclaimed. "What are you doing here?"

Pauline's eyes were red and swollen from crying. "She got a doctor to say I needed to be in a home, and then she dumped me," Pauline sobbed.

"Thank you, Nurse Swackhammer," I said as I knelt down by Pauline. "I'll take care of her."

"She's your client, too?" Nurse Swackhammer exclaimed in astonishment. Nurse Swackhammer left shaking her head as I wheeled Pauline over to the bed where we could sit and talk.

"Was it Jane, Pauline? Jane O'Donnel?"

Pauline nodded. "She had her attorney make out a new deed."

"You mean Aaron Longworth?" I asked.

Pauline nodded again.

"Why didn't you call me?"

"I was too ashamed. You and Freema were right. I never should have listened to her. Now I have nothing. My birds, everything … gone."

Pauline handed me her picture of Polyester. "How are you going to pay for your care?"

Pauline shrugged. "She said the government would be responsible."

"Pauline, Freema was telling me that Medicaid rules require that any assets given away within the last three years be given back before Medicaid will begin to pay for nursing home expenses. Didn't you tell Muffie Welsh about your house when you were admitted?"

Pauline shook her head, "Jane did all the talking."

I set the picture down on the table next to her. "Pauline, we may be able to make Jane give back all the money she made off your house, and we may even be able to get your house back as well."

Pauline's eyes grew hopeful. "Then you'll help me?"

"Of course I will. I'll do my best," I said, as I smiled and rubbed her frail little arm.

Just then, Willie appeared in the doorway with a food tray covered by a silver domed lid. He set it down beside her. "Here's your lunch."

"That should make you feel better," I said, trying to sound reassuring. "How about if I have Willie turn the TV on? That might get your mind off your troubles."

Willie complied and hit the remote. As luck would have it, he happened to turn to the scene from the 1960's Gothic horror movie, *What Ever Happened to Baby Jane?*, where a demented Bette Davis sets a tray of food down in front of Joan Crawford who is confined to a wheel chair. When an unsuspecting Joan removes the lid, she finds her dead parakeet which Bette has cooked with a lovely garnish.

I looked up in horror at Willie who had a very sadistic grin on his face. Grabbing the remote, I turned the TV off as Pauline started to cry again. It took a full 45 minutes before she was calm enough for me to leave her.

As I passed the chapel on my way out of the nursing home, I heard a woman sobbing uncontrollably. *Uh-oh*, I thought to myself, *Willie's been at it again*. The door was ajar, so I stuck my head in.

I was surprised to see Audrey, the nursing home aide, kneeling in prayer with her yellow rubber gloves sitting on the altar. I didn't know whether I should say anything, or to just try and sneak out unnoticed. Because Audrey seemed to be so distraught, I approached her from behind and lightly placed my hand on her shoulder.

"Audrey," I asked gently, "is something wrong?" When she looked up and saw it was me, she put her handkerchief up to her face and began to cry even harder.

"Look," I said, "if there's anything I can do to help …"

"There's nothing you can do," she cried as her body heaved. "There's nothing anyone can do now. It's too late for that."

I knelt down beside her. "It can't be all that bad," I said, trying to sound reassuring.

"Oh yes it can," came the reply. "God will never forgive me for what I've done."

"I don't know about that. Sometimes it just helps to talk things out. Remember, confession is good for the soul."

That was the wrong thing to say. Audrey looked at me and began sobbing again even more loudly than before. "Please," she begged, "please leave me alone. I just want to be alone …"

Realizing this was a lost cause, I got up, and tiptoed out of the chapel. Rounding a corner on my way out of the nursing home, I was glad to see Nurse Swackhammer enter Gretta's room. One encounter with her per visit was more than enough.

According to Nurse Swackhammer, the first thing she saw when she entered Gretta's room carrying her nurse's log were Rush's four little paws on the floor sticking straight out between the bed and the chair. Thinking he was asleep, she walked into the room, and turned Lawrence Welk down. Gretta had been playing it loudly enough to be heard in the next county. Nurse Swackhammer later told the authorities that it was when she turned around that she also saw Gretta lying on the floor, next to Rush.

"Gretta? Gretta?" Nurse Swackhammer screamed as she dropped her pad and attempted to revive Gretta with no immediate success. After what seemed an eternity, Gretta opened her eyes, reached up, and pointed to the table beside her chair. On it were the two pictures, the empty plate that had held my strudel, and the napkin that had held the fruitcake.

Nurse Swackhammer cradled Gretta in her arms. Gretta struggled to say something as she pointed to the table. Nurse Swackhammer put her ear down to Gretta's mouth. "Stru … stru … strudel." Gretta's arm dropped and she breathed her last as her lifeless body went limp in Nurse Swackhammer's arms. The nurse's eyes welled up with tears as she closed Gretta's eyelids.

An hour later, Maple Grove was pulling at the straps that were holding Gretta's blanket-covered corpse to a gurney while he busily smacked the two sticks of Juicy-Fruit gum he was chewing. Nearby, Muffie, who had morphed into a redhead, was prostrate with grief. She gently stroked Rush's sheet-covered body which was lying on a child-sized gurney. Dr. Thanatopsies was writing out a death certificate while Nurse Swackhammer looked on.

"What are you going to list as Gretta's cause of death?" Nurse Swackhammer inquired.

"Heart failure," the coroner replied mechanically.

Maple locked the legs of the gurney into place. "Good thing she prearranged her funeral."

"Heart failure!" Nurse Swackhammer exclaimed in disbelief as Maple signed for the body and wheeled Gretta out of the room. "In a pig's eye! How could she possibly have died from heart failure? She was the most active 87-year-old I've ever seen."

The doctor looked up from his black bag which he was packing. "Maybe she was … too active," he said, emphasizing the last two words for effect.

"Or maybe it wasn't heart failure that killed her!"

Nurse Swackhammer's retort caused the doctor to stop what he was doing and look at her intently. "What are you trying to say, Nurse Swackhammer?"

"Every time one of these old people dies," Nurse Swackhammer said, snapping her fingers for effect, "you write it off as heart failure. Well, I think they deserve more dignity than that! And I think the State Medical Board would agree with me. Besides, how do you explain Rush? The last one to see them both alive was that Sam Majors who brought Gretta some sort of apple strudel. Maybe he's responsible!" Now Nurse Swackhammer had Muffie's attention, too.

Dr. Thanatopsies shifted uncomfortably and then sighed with resignation. "All right, Nurse Swackhammer, if it'll make you feel better, I'll confirm it was heart failure before I issue the final death certificate."

Maple reappeared at the door and was preparing to remove Rush's gurney. Muffie grabbed his arm. "You will take care of my baby like we planned, won't you?"

"Like he was my very own," Maple replied reassuringly.

The Longworth law office was a scene of pandemonium as Aaron was attempting to supervise the workers who were trying to proceed with the remodeling job. Neville was searching for the ringing phone that could barely be heard above all the sawing and banging. Finally finding it under the architect's plans, he shouted, "Neville Longworth, here!"

Neville ducked just in time to avoid being hit by a plank a workman swung above his head. "What? You think there's been a murder?"

When another worker began to run a loud circular buzz saw, Aaron made him step aside so he could run it himself. Finally, Neville had enough and shouted at his father in exasperation, "Would you knock it off? There's been a murder!"

With that, the office fell deadly silent as everyone froze in their tracks and stared at the Prosecuting Attorney. A self-conscious Neville whispered into the phone, "I'll be right over."

The door to the Toxicology Lab at Dower County Hospital was ajar when Neville arrived. As soon as the stench of death hit him in the face, Neville became queasy. He hesitated before entering. He had never prosecuted a murder trial before and this was all new to him.

Dr. Thanatopsies was standing under a large vented hood with his back to the door. Nearby, Gretta lay face up on a table with a white sheet covering all but her face.

Neville cleared his throat several times to no avail. Glancing over nervously at the corpse, he tapped Dr. Thanatopsies on the shoulder. The doctor spun around on his heels.

He was wearing yellow rubber gloves, had a surgeon's mask over his nose and mouth and goggles over his eyes. In his hand he held a glass beaker full of brown gas that he had been heating over a Bunsen burner. The doctor put a stopper in the bottle.

Neville was taken aback. Dr. Thanatopsies held the beaker up in front of Neville's face. "Wha … what's that?"

When the doctor removed his mask, Neville could see he had those ever present flicks of dried foam around the edges of his mouth. Dr. Thanatopsies placed the goggles on his forehead, and with a fiendish gleam in his eye, whispered, "arsene."

Neville's eyes grew large as he stared at the gas. "Ar … arsene?"

"Yes," the doctor hissed. "A deadly gas I produced by heating the food in Gretta's …" He looked over at the corpse and hesitated for emphasis, "… stomach."

Neville's eyes traveled over to the corpse again. He gulped. "You … you mean she was poisoned?"

The doctor's eyes narrowed. "So it would seem," he said in a half whisper, half hiss.

"Wha … wha … what d … d … did sh … she eat?" Neville stammered.

"It appears to have been a combination of fruitcake they serve at the nursing home and some other sort of apple pastry that had been consumed contemporaneously. I can't tell which one had the poison in it," the doctor explained.

"I … I'd b, b, better ca, call the Sheriff," Neville said reaching for the phone.

"Not so fast," the doctor said as he placed his gloved hand over Neville's and forced the receiver down. "Not so fast. We wouldn't want to tip off the …"

He hesitated again for emphasis—"killer."

Unaware of what was unfolding at the hospital, I was back at the office going through the day's mail when the phone began to ring.

Freema answered it with her usual perky, "Margaret Majors' Office." I looked up at Freema curiously as her face fell and her voice grew flat. "Yes. He's here. Just a minute." She handed me the receiver and with as little enthusiasm as possible, said simply, "Hollywood calling collect."

My heart began to race as I put the receiver to my ear.

"He, hello?" I said haltingly. "Yes, I'll accept the charges. It's my agent!" I whispered excitedly to Freema who shrugged, unimpressed.

"You did? They did? You're kidding! I can't believe it!"

I cupped my hand over the phone again and half whispered, half shouted to Freema, "It's finally happened—my big break!" Freema shrugged and turned back to her work, pretending not to listen.

I put the phone back up to my ear. "Tomorrow? Of course I'll be there. I'll call you as soon as I get into town. All right, and thanks a million!"

I slammed the phone down and shouted, "One of the networks wants me to pitch my idea for a series to them!"

CHAPTER 14

"A murderer? Here at Buckeye Manor? Don't be ridiculous!" Muffie exclaimed between drags on her cigarette as she paced back and forth in her office.

"Then how do you explain the presence of arsenic in Mrs. Von Heimlich's stomach?" Neville demanded in his best prosecutorial manner. Dr. Thanatopsies smiled a wicked smile as Sheriff Weems, Detective Dewey Foltze and Muffie's husband, Jack, listened.

Nurse Swackhammer was just about to knock when she heard Muffie's voice through the door that was ajar. "But how could she have been poisoned? We maintain the highest of standards."

"Garden variety pesticide," Dr. Thanatopsies replied. "It appears to have been in something she ate just before she died." Nurse Swackhammer's jaw dropped open in shock and surprise. "I knew it!" Nurse Swackhammer said to herself.

"If word of this gets out, I'll be ruined!" Muffie cried. "Ma'am, do you keep any poison on the property?" Sheriff Weems asked.

"Of course not!" Muffie answered indignantly.

"What, what about the stuff you got for Ronnie to kill the rabbits with?" Jack Welsh asked meekly.

Muffie's glance shot daggers at her husband. "Quiet, Jack."

"I'd like to hear what your husband has to say," said the Sheriff. "Who's Ronnie?"

"My gardener. But he wouldn't hurt a fly!" Muffie shouted defensively as she ground out her cigarette in the ashtray.

"No one's saying he did, Ma'am. But just to be on the safe side, maybe we'd better do some checking," the Sheriff said as he looked to Detective Foltze for backup.

"Where is he now? Can we question him?" the detective asked.

"I sent him to town on an errand," Muffie replied hoping to stall for time. "He has to ride a bicycle because he doesn't drive, so it will be some time before he returns."

"I want to talk with him as soon as he is available," the Sheriff responded.

"Where is the poison kept and what kind is it?" inquired the Detective.

Jack started to answer, but Muffie cut him off. "We don't have time for this!"

"Then you'd better make time!" the Sheriff said with a hint of threat in his voice. "Now, let your husband answer the detective's question."

Muffie sighed. "Go ahead. Tell them, Jack."

"It's purchased downtown at the local hardware store. He keeps it in a locked closet. I think it's called *Insta-Death*. Yes, that's it. *Insta-Death.*"

"Appropriately named," Neville interjected with sarcasm in his voice.

"I want that closet dusted for fingerprints," the Sheriff ordered.

"Yes sir," the detective replied.

Muffie rose to her feet. "But the killer is still at large. What if he strikes again?" Muffie cried.

"What makes you so sure it's a man?" asked the Sheriff skeptically.

"I don't have time ..." Muffie started to say again before she caught herself. She threw herself down on a loveseat and lit another cigarette. "This can't be anything other than an isolated incident."

Dr. Thanatopsies advised, "I'm going to need more time to confirm my findings."

Out in the hall, Nurse Swackhammer had been taking down every word on the pad she kept with her at all times.

"Until he can be absolutely sure," Neville cautioned, "Dr. Thanatopsies wants to keep this quiet. I've agreed to go along, for now."

"Good, then it's settled," Muffie breathed with a sigh of relief.

"We'll see about that," Nurse Swackhammer said to herself, as she slipped away to avoid detection.

Very early the next day, I had driven myself to Detroit's Metro airport, blissfully unaware of events unfolding at home. I couldn't help but be aware of how different the weather conditions were compared to the night before Mom passed away when a blizzard almost kept me from returning to California. Ohio was experiencing a warm spell for the month of March. All the snow had melted and the temperature was up in the 50's. However, lightning and thunderstorms were forecast for later in the day, so I was anxious to get up in the air before they hit.

My mind was racing with excitement about the possibilities that lay ahead as I ate my lunch at one of those wonderful airport restaurants. I hoped my life's situation was beginning to thaw like the weather and that by spring all the angst I had experienced over the past six weeks would be as distant a memory as the icy cold weather.

What if my script gets produced?, I thought to myself. *Perhaps I'll win an Emmy! What would I say at the awards ceremony? Maybe that was too much to hope for right on my first effort. I'd settle for it just getting made. If it got picked up by one of the networks as a series, I'd have to relocate back to L.A., of course. I couldn't wait to see Marshall eat his words ...*

My happy little fantasy was interrupted when a news report on one of the airport restaurant's television monitors caught my eye. The reporter was doing a stand up in front of Buckeye Manor!

"An anonymous source has led to the discovery that one of the elderly residents in this Friendly, Ohio, nursing home may have been poisoned," the reporter said. Footage followed of Muffie driving up in her Jaguar, trying to shield her face as she tried to make her way through a crush of reporters. Normally, she would have loved the attention, but not this time.

The reporter continued, "The owner of the nursing home, Muffie Welsh, has refused comment. The name of the alleged victim is being withheld pending notification of the family."

What if it was Cora? I thought to myself. I tried to call Freema at the office, but both lines were busy.

Back at the nursing home, Muffie peered out from behind the curtain in her office at the reporters who filled the front lawn. Nearby, on her desk, sat her beloved Rush, stuffed and mounted by Maple, with a special added feature they had agreed on: a cigarette lighter in his head. Maple leaned over, pushed the lighter, and lit his cigar.

Muffie began to pace back and forth like a caged animal. She had called Neville, the Sheriff and Jack Welsh together for another meeting. Nurse Swackhammer had also been included for purposes of aiding in damage control. Maple happened to be there for one of his seminars, so Muffie had grabbed him on her way in for moral support. Up to then, he had no clue about what was going on.

"How in the hell did this get out?" Muffie demanded, looking accusatorially at Sheriff Weems. "You said we were gonna keep this quiet. Every damn reporter in the country must be out there!"

"Don't look at me, missy," the Sheriff countered.

"Then we must have a mole," Muffie replied, as Nurse Swackhammer tried to blend into the woodwork.

Dr. Thanatopsies knocked on the door. He was accompanied by Detective Foltze from the Sheriff's office. Muffie descended on them with the desperation of a drowning woman.

"Well? Well? Was it positive?"

"One hundred percent," said Dr. Thanatopsies. "The poison in the victim's body and the dog's is the same kind used by the gardener."

Muffie glared at her husband. "I told you we never should have hired that half-wit!"

Another knock was heard at the door, this time much more gentle than the detective's. "What is it!" Muffie barked.

The door slowly swung open and there stood Ronnie Trask. "You wanted to see me, Mrs. Welsh?" Ronnie asked meekly.

"The Sheriff wants to ask you some questions, Ronnie. Come in and sit down," Muffie directed as she motioned to a chair.

"Hi, Ronnie, I'm Sheriff Weems," the sheriff said gently as he began sizing Ronnie up.

As the sheriff stared at Ronnie, his right eye began to twitch, a sure sign he was becoming nervous. His agitation did not go unnoticed by the sheriff.

"Am I in trouble?" Ronnie asked, as he also began to bounce his right leg.

"No, son, are you nervous?" the Sheriff asked.

"No," Ronnie replied as he continued to twitch. "Well, maybe. Just a little."

"We wanted to talk with you because something bad may have happened here at the nursing home."

"Something bad?" Ronnie asked.

"Well, maybe. We aren't sure."

Ronnie looked at Muffie in a way that suggested he knew he had been discovered. Muffie's face registered no response.

"It has to do with some poison," the Sheriff continued.

"Poison?" Ronnie whispered as he looked down at the floor. Suddenly his eyes swelled up with tears and he began to sob. "I'm sorry," he cried. "I did it."

A look of horror passed across Muffie's face.

"Did what, son?" the Sheriff asked gently.

"I killed them. I killed all of them," Ronnie cried between sobs.

"I knew it!" Muffie shouted angrily.

Sheriff Weems held up his hand to her to be quiet with a look that communicated he meant business.

"They didn't hurt anyone. I didn't want to kill them, but Mrs. Welsh told me I had to."

"Why you lying little son of a bitch!" Muffie shouted.

"And then I cut off their feet," Ronnie continued.

A look of horror passed across everyone's face except for Maple who leaned forward with great interest as he exclaimed, "A foot fetish?"

The Sheriff held up his hand again to regain control. "What are you talking about, son?"

"Those bunnies. I didn't want to kill them, but Mrs. Welsh said I had to or they'd chew off her trees."

"Rabbits?" Muffie shouted. "This is all about some damn rabbits?"

The Sheriff took Ronnie's rabbit's feet necklace in his hands. Are these the feet you were talking about?"

"Yeah," Ronnie replied. "That's part of them."

The Sheriff grinned as he looked at the others. There was an audible sigh of relief in the room.

"They're mighty fine specimens, son. I had a collection like that when I was young, too."

"You did?" Ronnie asked.

"I sure did," Sheriff Weems replied. "Tell me, Ronnie, have you ever used the poison for anything else?"

Ronnie looked up at the Sheriff with an expression of innocence which lacked any guile. His eye had stopped twitching and his leg was still.

"No, sir," he replied in earnest.

"Well, that does it for me," Sheriff Weems said. "Mr. Prosecutor?"

Neville nodded and the Sheriff told Ronnie he could leave.

After Ronnie had left Muffie's office, Detective Foltze stepped forward. "Sheriff Weems, there is something else you should know. When we dusted the gardener's closet, we found two sets of fingerprints."

"Two?" Muffie asked with surprise.

"Those of Ronald Trask, whose prints we obtained from him voluntarily, and the others belonging to one Samuel P. Majors."

Everyone was thunderstruck.

"Sam Majors?" Muffie asked.

"The attorney?"

The Sheriff looked perplexed. "Margaret Majors' son?"

"His fingerprints were still in the State's registry from when he took the bar exam," the detective interjected.

"But why would he …" the Sheriff began to ask when he was interrupted by Neville who looked as if he had just received an epiphany.

"Who was Mrs. Von Heimlich's attorney?"

Nurse Swackhammer's eyes grew large as she shouted, "Sam Majors!"

Neville smiled and nodded. "And he stood to gain a lot by probating the victim's estate."

The Sheriff shook his head as he rubbed the back of his neck. "Those are pretty serious charges. You'd better have some damn good evidence before you start making those kinds of allegations."

"How do you account for finding his fingerprints in the gardener's closet, then?" Neville asked.

Nurse Swackhammer chimed in. "And I was with Gretta when she died. The last word out of her mouth was "strudel," just after Sam Majors had brought her some."

"Some what?" Neville asked.

"Some apple strudel," Nurse Swackhammer said condescendingly.

Muffie's eyes narrowed as her face became contorted with the look of vengeance. "If he's the one who poisoned my little Rush, he's going to wish he'd never been born!"

"Could it be any coincidence that Opal Thomas, Rachel McDowell and Esther Dale were his clients also and now they're dead too?" Nurse Swackhammer asked.

"You mean he could be a serial killer?" Muffie asked in horror.

"That's what I'd call him!" replied Nurse Swackhammer.

The Sheriff looked at Maple Grove. "I think we'd better ask the court for authority to exhume their remains."

Maple gulped as he looked at Dr. Thanatopsies whose face registered no response. "Uh, I don't think that will be possible," Maple said nervously.

"What he means to say," interjected the doctor, "is that they've already been cremated."

"Well, in any case, I want to get Sam Majors in for questioning. Take care of it!" the Sheriff ordered Detective Foltze, who had already dialed the phone on Muffie's desk and was waiting for Freema to answer.

"None of this started to happen until he came back. I never did trust him … nosin' around here like a hog at the …" Nurse Swackhammer stopped short when she realized Muffie did not appreciate her analogy.

"It's obvious he had the most to gain," Neville observed.

"Now let's not jump to any conclusions," said Sheriff Weems. "A man is innocent until …"

"What the hell do you mean he's left town?" the Detective shouted into the phone.

At Detroit Metro, I finished my lunch and decided I'd go to my gate to try and call Freema again to find out if she knew what was going on at Buckeye Manor. As I waited for her to answer, I heard my name being paged. Suddenly, I felt a large hand over mine forcing the receiver back to its cradle. I turned around to see it was the Wayne County Sheriff, along with a television camera crew. The Dower County Sheriff had contacted the local sheriff to track me down through my airline reservation. I was not only confused, but frightened about what it all meant.

I was placed in a secure room at the airport until the Dower County Sheriff could arrive. I was totally at a loss as to what was happening because the authorities wouldn't tell me anything.

It was after 6:00 p.m. when the Dower County Sheriff finally showed up. Despite my protestations, I was hustled from the airport into the back of the Sheriff's cruiser. It wasn't until we were on the Interstate heading South back to Friendly that I learned I was wanted for questioning in Gretta Von Heimlich's murder.

When the Sheriff told me, I was dumbfounded. Remembering my Miranda rights, I sat in stony silence the rest of the two-hour ride home.

That night, residents at the nursing home were crowded around a television watching my life go up in flames on a tabloid news program. "They call him the Probate Piranha," the reporter said with staccato machine gun-like alliteration. "A predator-like attorney who allegedly poisoned his wealthy elderly clients so he could profit from probating their estates ..."

Footage of Buckeye Manor flashed on the screen. "The scene of the crime was this picturesque Victorian mansion in Friendly, Ohio, which looks like a place Norman Rockwell might have dreamed up, where sweet unsuspecting residents thought they would be well taken care of ..."

"They were taken care of all right. It is alleged that these elderly women" (pictures of Rachel, Opal and Esther flashed on the screen, followed by Rush), "and this dog, may have been poisoned by this man whose motive is believed to have been money."

The report cut to a dorky picture of me from my high school yearbook. "Sam Majors, whose fourth alleged victim, Gretta Von Heimlich ..."

The report cut to a picture of Gretta. "... is the only one of his alleged victims whose body was not cremated prior to the discovery of his sinister plan ..."

A toothless Mr. Nofzinger was sitting front and center in the TV lounge at Buckeye Manor. Raising his cane in rage he shouted, "I hope they fry the bastard!" Other residents grumbled in chorus, with the exception of one individual, who remained stone-faced.

Footage of a very bewildered looking me being arrested and cuffed at Detroit Metropolitan Airport flashed on the screen. "The alleged perpetrator of these heinous crimes was arrested this afternoon on suspicion of murder as he was boarding a flight for Los Angeles on the first leg of what is believed to have been his plan to have plastic surgery before assuming a new identity ..."

The thunderstorm which enveloped us as we drove back to Friendly, seemed to symbolize what was happening in my life. As we entered the city limits, I saw the familiar greeting which read:

WELCOME HOME
TO
FRIENDLY!

How ironic, I mused. Suddenly, a huge bolt of lightning hit the sign. *Somebody up there doesn't like me*, I thought to myself. The sandstone peaks and brick arches of the ancient Dower County Jail were illuminated by lightning as Sheriff Weems pulled up to it with me in the back of his cruiser. Neville had persuaded the court to issue a warrant for my arrest on the probable cause of murder. I'll bet he just hated doing that.

Rain pelted my face as the deputy pulled me from the back of the cruiser in handcuffs. A crush of reporters surged forward, their camera lights and flashes blinding me as they shoved their microphones in my face. Law enforcement in Friendly wasn't as media savvy as their Detroit counterparts.

"Did you do it? Are you guilty? Were there others?" These were just a few of the questions they shouted. Every time I'd try to say I was innocent, thunder would drown me out. After what seemed forever, Sheriff Weems finally rescued me and dragged me through the gate of the ancient black wrought iron fence and into the jail where he turned me over to a deputy to be booked and fingerprinted.

Holding those serial numbers under my chin as they photographed me made me feel like I was an observer watching this happening to someone else. It reminded me of the way I had felt walking through the airport on my way home after getting the news that Mom had died. This couldn't really be happening; it was only a bad dream and I was going to wake up at any moment.

Suddenly Tori burst in dripping wet from the rain, her clothes clinging tightly to her shapely body. She grabbed my shoulders and embraced me. "Are you okay? I came as soon as I heard!"

"Tori! How'd you get in here?"

She grinned and whispered in my ear. "I told them I was your sister."

"Hi, Sis," I said hugging her tightly. Seeing her there, all dripping wet, with her body pressed close to mine, was just what I needed. Despite the fact I was being booked for murder, I was starting to get turned on. I felt a sudden surge of confidence.

"Remember how I told you I felt like a prison door was closing shut on me? Well, now it's really happened, and it's all because I'm being framed for something I didn't do!"

"I know you're innocent!" she replied.

"This is all Neville's doing. That son-of-a-bitch! He's been jealous of me from the start."

"You mean of us …" Tori replied.

That revelation caught me off guard. "Of us? Really?" I said with a big grin.

"Yes, really!" Tori replied. "I told him how much courage I thought it took for you to give up all your dreams and come back here like you did …" And then she kissed me, in a way one wouldn't expect to be kissed by one's sister.

"I hate to break up this little family reunion …" the deputy said sarcastically as he began to pull me away.

"Really?" I said again, grinning from ear to ear. Tori nodded and I was smiling when the deputy led me through the first of a series of doors.

I pulled back on the bars of the door which closed with a heavy clang. For somebody behind bars, I sure felt free.

"I believe in you!" she shouted after me.

After being fingerprinted, they ordered me to strip and put on a suit of black and white stripes which featured in large black letters the words: *Dower County Department of Corrections.* I thought stripes had gone out with the chain gangs. Apparently not in Friendly.

They led me down a narrow set of concrete stairs into the dark dank dungeon that made up the bowels of the Dower

County Jail. The walls, into which generations had carved their names, were made of brick three feet thick. The air smelled damp and musty. I was glad Opal had left her money to build a new jail, but I wished somebody else had done it sooner.

We arrived at my cell, which seemed strangely familiar. The big heavy iron bars swung open with a huge groan as the deputy pushed me in.

And suddenly, I was five again. Franklin was 10 and Marshall was 12. Mom was Juvenile Judge. She and Dad were still married. They must have thought they needed to make an impression on those little hellians, the Majors boys, so they took us down to the jail, had a deputy put us in that very cell, and closed the door. Then they said, "Now, boys, don't ever do anything that will cause you to end up here." Then they let us out and gave us all cards and badges signifying we were junior deputies. We got the message. I wondered what my mother would have said if she could have seen me now.

The heavy door swung shut with a clang. There was a legend surrounding that particular cell which was why I recognized it immediately. On the wall were gouges that had supposedly been made by a prisoner trying to claw his way out when they were coming to take him to the gallows. Pretty unbelievable, unless you're a five-year-old boy at the mercy of his two older brothers.

Lightning flashed and thunder cracked outside the ground level basement window as the rain continued to come down in torrents. The deputy sat down at his desk, put his feet up, and turned to an oldies station on his radio. As if to put the finishing touch on the already unbelievable series of events unfolding before me, Gene Pitney wailed, "It Isn't Very Pretty What a Town Without Pity Can Do." I couldn't have agreed more as I closed my eyes and slid down the wall to the floor, surrendering to complete and total exhaustion.

CHAPTER 15

My probable cause-and-bail hearing had been set for the next day at 3 p.m. After trying to reach Marshall all morning by phone, he finally answered about 10:30. "Where the hell have you been?" I shouted into the receiver of the deputy's desk phone which barely reached through the bars of my cell.

Marshall was busy eating an Egg McMuffin. "I've been out trapping," he said perfunctorily between bites. "What's wrong?"

"I've only been arrested and charged with murder, that's all!"

"What?" Marshall replied as he choked on his sandwich. Apparently he hadn't been near a television in the last 24 hours.

"You know those sweet little old ladies you said I'd make a fortune taking care of? Well, the Dower County Prosecutor says I poisoned four of them!"

"That's ridiculous!" Marshall scoffed, as the deputy reached through the bars to take the phone receiver.

"Time's up, Buddy!"

"Listen, Marshall," I said. "You and Frank got me into this. Now you'd better damn well come down here and get me out!"

"Don't worry, Little Brother, I'm on my way," Marshall assured me as the deputy took the phone from my hands.

"Best damn door in the whole ..." Aaron Longworth was standing next to his new walnut office door, bragging to his secretaries when it flew open, pinning him behind it in the corner.

Freema stood there like a wounded bear whose cub had been attacked. "Where's Aaron?" Freema demanded. "I know he's behind this!" The secretaries looked nonplussed, as one pointed and motioned behind the door.

"Whaddya think of my new door? I installed it myself!" Aaron bellowed from behind his walnut masterpiece.

Freema grabbed the big brass door knob and flung it closed loudly enough that Aaron knew she meant business.

"Well, a simple 'I don't like it' would have sufficed," Aaron said with feigned innocence.

Much to the amazement of Aaron's secretaries, Freema backed him into the corner. "Don't play dumb with me, Aaron Longworth! I know you're behind what Neville's doing to Sam."

Aaron shrugged as he brushed past her and flopped himself down in an easy chair, his leg over the arm.

Freema got right in his face as she poked him in the shoulder with her finger. "I always knew you wanted Margaret's practice, but I never thought you'd stoop to something this low to get it! Before Margaret went to the hospital, I promised her that if anything happened to her and Sam ever came back, I'd stay long enough to help him get started. As long as I'm here, Margaret's still here, and that means you have one hell of a fight on your hands!"

Before Aaron could reply, Freema stormed out of the office, flinging the door open so hard it broke loose from the hinges and came crashing to the floor. Aaron had to jump out of the chair to avoid being hit. He turned and glowered at his secretaries who were trying hard not to erupt in laughter. "What the hell you lookin' at? Get back to work!"

Because Neville believed the combination of the discovery of my fingerprints in the gardener's closet, along with Gretta's last utterance were such strong evidence, he had decided to forego a grand jury indictment and charge me directly.

Since I was a member of the local bar, our Common Pleas Judge had recused himself from hearing my case. In his place had been assigned Terrence Bexley, a visiting Judge from Cuyahoga County. Judge Bexley was known across the State as "The Grim Reaper" for his sullen demeanor and ardent support of maximum sentencing, which in the case of capital crimes, usually meant the death penalty. If that wasn't bad enough, he was running for a spot on the Ohio Supreme Court and the May primary was looming on the horizon. Mine was sure to be a high profile trial. The only thing I had going for me was the fact that Judge Bexley had been a senior partner in my brother Marshall's firm before taking the bench.

The press had all been waiting for me like vultures outside the jail. The Sheriff sneaked me out the back and drove me around the block to the courthouse in an unmarked car. Thanks to Marshall's insistence, I had been allowed to exchange my black and white stripes for blue pin stripes.

The courtroom was like a zoo when the deputy ushered me in, chained and shackled. The clicking of cameras echoed off the tall, cold walls. The media was assembled at the back of the courtroom. It was standing room only.

I took my place next to Marshall at the defense table. Freema, Franklin and Tori were seated behind us in the gallery. Neville was seated to our right at the Prosecutor's table. He tried to make eye contact with Tori, but she turned and looked the other way. He was not happy.

The bailiff walked in and bellowed "all rise" and everyone stood to their feet. "Oyez, Oyez, Oyez! The Common Pleas

Court of Dower County is now in session. His Honor, Judge Terrence Bexley, of the Cuyahoga County Common Pleas Court now presiding."

Judge Bexley entered from the Judge's chamber located behind the bench and surveyed the situation. He was an imposing figure—intimidating is a better description—standing 6'5″ in flowing black robes, silver hair and a glowering expression only Nurse Swackhammer could appreciate.

The Judge was just about to bring down his gavel when the large double doors to the courtroom swung open, followed by a putt-putt-putt, as Aaron Longworth rode his moped into the courtroom. For this special occasion, he had attached a White Castle Hamburger Restaurant flag to a tall orange plastic pole extending up from his rear axle.

The gallery of onlookers erupted in fits of laughter. These were still the days before the Supreme Court of Ohio had mandated courthouse security. Virtually anyone could have entered under just about any circumstances, and Friendly was still a small town whose citizens took a dim view of too much regulation.

Marshall and I looked at each other in disbelief. Neville was horrified. I thought I detected just the hint of amusement on the Judge's face.

"Hiya, Judge!" Aaron bellowed as he waved and circled in front of the bench before stopping.

Marshall leaned over and whispered in my ear, "They graduated from law school together."

Great!, I thought to myself, *My goose is really cooked.*

The smile on the Judge's face passed as quickly as it came. "Order! Order!" Judge Bexley bellowed as he banged his gavel trying to regain control. "I will not have this courtroom turned into a circus!"

Pointing his gavel at Aaron, he shouted, "Mr. Longworth, your antics may be tolerated down here, but where I come from, they are grounds for discipline. Any more shenanigans like this, and I will be talking to the State Bar Association. Now get out of here before I hold you in contempt!"

"Sorry, Judge!" Aaron replied unfazed, as he winked at the spectators, waved, and putt-putt-putted out of the courtroom and into a waiting elevator across the hall.

"Judge," Neville groveled, "I am very sorry ..."

Judge Bexley held up his hand to stop him. "Mr. Longworth, I am not excusing his behavior, but I have known your father for a very long time. Let's get on with matters at hand."

The Judge reviewed the sealed indictment and the charges Neville had filed against me. Fixing his penetrating gaze on me, he said, "Mr. Majors, as I am sure you are aware, the charges against you are serious—very serious. We are here today to hold a preliminary hearing to determine if there is probable cause for charging you with murder."

I nodded in silent understanding as my palms began to sweat and my throat closed. Marshall gripped my arm in assurance.

"Mr. Longworth," Judge Bexley continued, "The People may proceed."

"Your Honor," Neville pontificated with as much drama as he was capable of mustering, "the good People of Dower County intend to establish sufficient probable cause to bind the Defendant, Samuel P. Majors, over to the Court of Common Pleas to be tried for the murder of one Gretta Von Heimlich. A murder he perpetrated in a cold and calculated manner by poisoning her with the motive of profiting from probating her estate. Circumstantial evidence points to Mr. Majors as the chief suspect, the only suspect, who had both the motive and the opportunity to commit this heinous crime. He was the last person to see the alleged victim, and ..."

As the Judge rolled his eyes, Marshall jumped to his feet. "Your Honor, we object! Mr. Longworth is testifying ..."

Judge Bexley barked at Neville, "Mr. Longworth, the court is well aware why we are here. Now get on with presenting your evidence." Neville withered and began to squirm.

"Your Honor, the People had hoped to call as its first witness the Dower County Coroner, Dr. Homer Thanatopsies." Neville surveyed the courtroom one last time. "But it appears he has been detained. Therefore, the people call Nurse Etta Swackhammer."

The bailiff escorted Nurse Swackhammer from the witness room where she had been waiting. She approached the witness stand carrying a large black valise, wearing a crisp white, newly-pressed nurse's uniform, a nurse's hat neatly pinned atop her head, and newly polished white shoes. All business, as usual. Her appearance and demeanor certainly did lend credibility to her image as a competent nurse.

After the preliminaries, Neville asked her to tell the court what she had observed. "Well, on the day in question …"

"You mean the day Mrs. Von Heimlich died?" Neville interrupted.

Marshall jumped to his feet. "Objection, your Honor! He's leading the witness."

"I'll rephrase," Neville responded before Judge Bexley could reply. "What day was that, Nurse Swackhammer?"

Nurse Swackhammer looked knowingly at the judge. "Why, March 10, 1989, the day Mrs. Von Heimlich died, of course. I was working at the front desk when he …" she said, pointing an accusatory finger in my direction …

"You mean the defendant, Sam Majors?" Neville asked.

"Yes, him," Nurse Swackhammer replied solicitously, still pointing her long bony finger in my direction.

"Let the record reflect the witness has identified the defendant, Sam Majors," Neville interjected. "You may continue, Nurse Swackhammer."

"When Sam Majors walked into the nursing home carrying what he told me was apple strudel for Mrs. Von Heimlich. After he signed in, which is, by the way, our usual custom …"

Neville interrupted. "Do you have that register with you today?"

"Why yes. Yes I do." Nurse Swackhammer pulled the register out of the valise, opened it, and pointed to the place where I had signed it.

Neville examined the register and handed it to my brother for his examination. Marshall handed it back to Neville who presented it to Judge Bexley. "We would like to have this marked as *People's Exhibit 1*."

The Judge examined the register and handed it to the Bailiff to enter the register as evidence, after which it was handed back to Neville.

"And when does the register reflect Mr. Majors signed in?" Neville asked Nurse Swackhammer as he handed her the register.

"7:10 p.m.," she replied, "March 10, 1989, on the day Mrs. Von Heimlich was murdered."

"Objection!" Marshall shouted.

The Judge sighed. Nurse Swackhammer, please restrict your comments only to facts of which you have personal knowledge."

Nurse Swackhammer glared at me while speaking with feigned innocence. "I'm sorry, your Honor, that's what I thought I was doing."

"You may continue," Judge Bexley instructed.

"After authorities made the connection between Mrs. Von Heimlich's death and Mr. Majors, I went back and checked my register. Every day Mr. Majors came to visit one of his clients, they seemed to develop another mysterious case of heart failure."

Marshall jumped to his feet, this time with pained exasperation in his voice, "Your Honor ..."

Before Neville could reply, the Judge ordered that Nurse Swackhammer's last comment be stricken from the record, assured everyone that he was the trier of fact, and that I was innocent until proven guilty.

Neville continued. "After Mr. Majors signed the register, what did he do next?"

"I watched him as he walked toward Mrs. Von Heimlich's room. She was sitting in her favorite easy chair, watching Lawrence Welk, and holding the nursing home mascot, Rush ..."

Marshall jumped to his feet. "Unless Nurse Swackhammer had a clear line of vision, how could she know where Mrs. Von Heimlich was sitting or whether she had the dog on her lap?"

The Judge looked at Neville. "Well, Mr. Longworth?"

Neville looked at Nurse Swackhammer who clearly appeared shaken by the continued interruption of her well-rehearsed narrative. She squirmed, shifting uncomfortably in the witness seat, "That was where I had observed her just prior to Mr. Majors entering the nursing home, and she hadn't left her room and the TV was turned up loud enough so I could hear ..."

Judge Bexley interrupted. "The record will reflect that prior to the defendant entering the nursing home, the witness observed the deceased sitting in her chair. You may continue Nurse Swackhammer."

Nurse Swackhammer managed a smile for the Judge. It was the first I'd ever seen pass across her face. "I went on about my work, but sometime later, I would judge to be 15 minutes or so, I was making my usual rounds. When I entered Mrs. Von Heimlich's room, I saw Rush lying on the floor. This was nothing unusual and I assumed he was asleep."

As the drama in Nurse Swackhammer's voice began to mount, I wondered how much embellishment was going on.

"The television had been turned up very loud, and when I went to turn it down, I found Mrs. Von Heimlich lying on the floor, clutching at her throat. I managed to revive her, but I was too late. All she whispered was one word, 'strudel,' and then both she and Rush were gone." At this point, Nurse Swackhammer's eyes welled up with tears.

"You mean the dog died, too?" the Judge asked.

"Yes, your Honor. I brought him along if you'd like to see him."

The Judge's eyes grew large. "You mean you brought a dead dog into the courtroom? Is ... is he in that valise?"

Nurse Swackhammer nodded tearfully as she pulled him from the black bag.

"If he died at the same time as Mrs. Von Heimlich, doesn't he ..." the Judge hesitated, searching for the proper word, "smell?"

Nurse Swackhammer placed Rush on the bench in front of the Judge. "No, your Honor. Mrs. Welsh, she runs the nursing home, Mrs. Welsh had him stuffed immediately so we could have him with us always."

"No further questions of this witness, your Honor," Neville declared victoriously, but the Judge didn't seem to hear. He was fascinated by the stuffed dog.

I whispered in Marshall's ear that "strudel" was also Gretta's pet name for her boyfriend, Harold Hardesty.

Like a boy with a new toy, the Judge was still engrossed in Rush. He looked it over carefully until he came to the cigarette lighter in the head. He bent over it with a quizzical expression on his face. He pushed the lighter a couple of times until a large flame shot out which I suspect probably singed his eyebrows. The courtroom erupted in laughter as Judge Bexley jumped back. Things quieted quickly upon his ominous glare.

"Nurse Swackhammer," Marshall asked, "isn't it a fact that Mrs. Von Heimlich had a gentleman friend whom she occasionally referred to as her "strudel"?

"If she did," Nurse Swackhammer replied innocently, "I wasn't aware of it."

Despite all my training, I could contain myself no longer. I jumped up and shouted, "That's a damn lie! She knew everything that went on at that nursing home."

Judge Bexley banged his gavel and told Marshall in no uncertain terms that any more such outbursts and he would have me removed from the courtroom. Neville just stood there and smirked, gratified that he had gotten me to lose my cool.

"Mr. Majors?" the Judge asked Marshall. My brother shook his head "no" as he whispered in my ear, "I know how you feel, but don't worry, Sam. This is nothing more than a preliminary hearing. We'll have our chance." I was beginning to have my doubts. I'd heard of people who felt they'd been railroaded by the system, but I never thought it would happen to me.

The bailiff handed the judge a note and whispered something in his ear. His face registered shock and surprise.

"What?" he asked the bailiff to repeat what he had told him to make sure he had heard correctly.

The Judge looked at Neville and Marshall. "It appears there has been another suspicious death at the nursing home. A Mr. Nofzinger."

"That man wasn't one of my clients!" I blurted out.

"Your Honor! Your Honor!" Both Marshall and Neville vied to be the first to respond to this revelation. The crowd and the media erupted in pandemonium as the Judge once again attempted to regain order. Looking at Marshall, Judge Bexley motioned for him to speak first.

"Your Honor, it would have been impossible for my client to have been involved in this man's death, since he was already in custody. In light of this recent development, I request that the Court order an immediate autopsy."

"You're too late," hissed a voice from the back of the courtroom.

Everyone turned to see Dr. Thanatopsies standing at the back of the courtroom, dressed in a white lab coat, wearing yellow rubber gloves and holding a beaker with a stopper in it.

"I presume you are Dr. Thanatopsies?" Judge Bexley asked. "Precisely," the doctor replied, "Dr. LeRoy Thanatopsies."

"You may approach the bench, sir. Bailiff, swear him in." Dr. Thanatopsies took the stand.

After Neville was done qualifying Dr. Thanatopsies as to his credentials, Judge Bexley leaned forward and asked with great curiosity, "What do you have there, doctor?"

Dr. Thanatopsies held the beaker up and swirled its contents. "Arsene," he hissed in a whisper.

"I beg your pardon?" asked the Judge, somewhat taken aback by the doctor's ghoulish manner.

"Arsene," Dr. Thanatopsies repeated, "made from cooking the contents found in the stomach of ..." he hesitated for emphasis, "... the late Mr. Nofzinger."

"And your findings?" Judge Bexley inquired in a courtroom so quiet you could have heard a pin drop.

"Oscar Nofzinger died after eating fruitcake laced with arsenic, the same kind of poison found mixed in with the food in the stomach of Mrs. Von Heimlich."

"Can you be more specific as to the nature of the poison?" Neville probed.

"It appears to be an ordinary arsenic-based poison that could be purchased anywhere for eliminating garden variety pests."

"And how much of this poison would it take to kill a person?"

"A very small amount! Say one-eighth of a teaspoon, would be enough to stop a person's heart from beating," the Dr. replied.

"And what kind of food was found in the stomach of the deceased?" Neville continued.

"You are referring to the food in the stomach of Mrs. Von Heimlich?" the Dr. asked.

"Yes," Neville replied.

"There was the same sort of fruitcake that is served at the nursing home that was found in the stomach of Oscar Nofzinger, as well as what appeared to be something made with apples such as pie, or possibly strudel. The two had been ingested simultaneously, so it was impossible for me to tell which had contained the poison."

A slight murmur arose which the Judge quickly quelled. The Judge looked at me. "And you say this Mr. Nofzinger wasn't one of your clients, Mr. Majors?"

"I've never met the man in my life, your Honor," I said with certainty.

"But Your Honor," Neville squealed with that high-pitched whine that let you know he knew he was in trouble, "his fingerprints ..."

Judge Bexley interrupted him. "Are you resting, Mr. Longworth?"

Neville appeared momentarily fazed. "No. No, your Honor. The People call Detective Dewey Foltze to the stand."

The bailiff retrieved the deputy from the witness room. After the preliminaries of the swearing in and qualifying the witness, Neville got right to the point. "Detective Foltze, in the course of your investigation, were you able to ascertain whether poison was used at the nursing home where the alleged victim lived?"

"Yes," Detective Foltze replied.

"For what purpose, Detective?"

"It is used on the flower beds."

"And what is the brand?"

"*Insta-Death*."

"Appropriately named." Neville looked at me with revulsion as he played to the press and gallery. "And where was this poison kept at the nursing home?"

Marshall objected again, stating that the detective was not qualified to testify where the poison was kept at the nursing home. Judge Bexley sustained the objection and Neville asked the court for indulgence assuring the Judge that his next inquiry would clarify where this line of questioning was leading. The Judge told him he was on a short leash, but could continue.

"And where was this poison kept, Detective Foltze?"

"In the gardener's closet," came the reply.

"Did you find any fingerprints in the gardener's closet, Detective Foltze?"

"Yes," the Detective replied.

"And whose were they?"

"Objection!" Marshall shouted. "Mr. Longworth is leading the witness!"

"Sustained," Judge Bexley ruled.

"I will rephrase, your Honor. Neville thought a moment as he regrouped. "Detective, did you dust the gardener's closet for fingerprints?"

"Yes."

"And whose fingerprints did you find?"

Marshall looked at me quizzically as to whether I had any idea where this was heading. I shrugged and shook my head.

"There were only two sets of prints. Those of the gardener, Ronald Trask, and those of the defendant, Samuel P. Majors."

The courtroom erupted in chaos again at this revelation. Marshall looked at me and I came up blank, until I remembered the day at the nursing home I'd entered the gardener's closest because I'd heard something fall and was afraid it was one of the residents. Judge Bexley pounded his gavel and warned everyone that he would clear the courtroom in the event of any more outbursts.

"The People rest, your Honor." Neville sat down and crossed his arms with a smile of self-satisfaction.

Judge Bexley looked at Marshall. "Mr. Majors, you may proceed."

"The defense will waive presentation of its evidence, your Honor."

I grabbed Marshall's arm. "What do you mean, Marshall? Aren't you going to present anything on my behalf?"

"No, not now," Marshall whispered in my ear. "I don't want to give away anything now that Neville may try to use later at the trial." I was totally clueless as to what was going on at this point, but I knew I had to trust my brother.

"Then the defense rests?" the Judge asked.

"Yes, your Honor."

"Very well. While the revelation of this recent death does raise some interesting questions, it appears that Mr. Majors had both the motive and the opportunity to have committed the crime with which he has been charged. Therefore, it is the finding of this court that probable cause does exist for charging the Defendant, Samuel P. Majors, with the murder of Gretta Von Heimlich, and it is hereby Ordered that he be bound over for trial." The Judge's solemn demeanor as he made his finding kept the viewing public in check.

The Judge looked at Marshall. "Mr. Majors, do you intend to ask that your brother be released on bail pending trial?"

Before Marshall could answer, Neville interrupted, "If that is the case, your Honor, we would ask the court to set bail at a minimum of $500,000, cash."

The Judge frowned at Neville for his lack of professional courtesy.

Marshall jumped to his feet. "Your Honor, the Prosecutor's request is both excessive and unwarranted by the facts ..."

"On the contrary, your Honor," Neville interrupted again.

The Judge looked at Marshall. "Mr. Majors, would it be your intention to have this court believe your brother is not a flight risk, when he was at the Detroit airport when apprehended while preparing to board a flight to Los Angeles?"

"But I wasn't ..." was all I managed to get out before the Judge held his hand up as he leaned back in his chair, rubbed his chin, and stared at the ornate plaster cherubs on the ceiling of the ancient courtroom.

Finally, after what seemed like forever, he fixed a studied gaze upon me and asked, "Mr. Majors, how much do you stand to earn from the estates of the clients who have died since you came back to Friendly?"

I was at a loss. I looked back at Freema for guidance. After some quick calculations on her part, she leaned over the rail and whispered something in my ear. I gulped at the sum. I never had any idea.

I turned back toward the judge, cleared my throat, and in a voice which I hoped was audible only to the Judge, murmured, "a hundred thousand dollars."

"What was that? Speak up, Mr. Majors," Judge Bexley demanded. I cleared my throat again, and said it loudly enough so that he could hear.

"One hundred thousand dollars, your Honor." A gasp swept through the courtroom.

Freema leaned over the rail and grabbed my collar. "Tell him that is just an estimate according to the probate court's own fee guidelines, but that you would reduce it."

"But that's based upon the probate court's own fee guidelines," I added. "I could always reduce it."

Unfortunately, that last little tidbit of information was lost on the courtroom.

"A hundred thousand, eh? Not bad for a couple of month's work. Bail is set at one hundred thousand dollars. Court adjourned!"

Judge Bexley banged his gavel one last time and all the emotion which Judge Bexley had tried so hard to suppress in his courtroom was finally set free.

The bailiff led me out as Marshall left to arrange for my bail. Tori made her way over to Neville. I didn't see it, but Freema told me she watched Tori dump Neville right then and there. For once, Neville was speechless.

Marshall, God bless him, put up his own money to pay for my bail. When I opened the big walnut doors of the courthouse to exit, I noticed a huge crowd of spectators at the bottom of the limestone steps. They'd been unable to get into court for my hearing and were milling about restlessly along with a media circus mob.

Protestors, malcontents and other assorted disgruntled geriatrics were holding signs which read "*Euthanize All Lawyers!*" "*Probate the S.O.B.,*" "*Death Is Too Good For Him,*" and, "*Go Back To The Land Of Fruits And Nuts!*"

But the one that really caught my attention was carried by none other than Aaron Longworth who was front and center, gleefully enjoying the circus atmosphere. His sign read, "*Neville Knows Best!*"

When I saw that, something inside me snapped. It was my moment of epiphany. Like the Grinch whose heart finally grew, I suddenly found my backbone. Up to that point, I had been the victim, but no more. I was, after all, Margaret Majors' son. She had been a fighter, and pushed to the wall, I could be one too. "Neville knows best!" I shouted ballistically. "Well, I'll be damned. If that son-of-a-bitch thinks he's gonna get rid of me that easy, he's got another damn thing coming!"

I was ready to start down the stairs, when Marshall pulled me back through the door. "Don't lower yourself to his level, Sam. That's exactly what he wants," which is the same thing our mother would have said. "Go back inside, Sam, I'll take care of this crowd."

In my heart, I knew he was right. After a moment's hesitation, I stepped back through the door and let him go ahead.

I had just shut the door, when I felt the gentle touch of a warm hand on my back. "What are we gonna do now?"

I turned around. It was Tori. "We?" I asked.

"Yeh," she smiled, "as in you and me."

"But you're dating Neville, and he just happens to be the enemy right now. Don't you think that presents a conflict of interest?"

"Not anymore."

"You mean you …?"

Tori nodded and smiled. "I had to return a bad barrel of apples."

"Huh?" I asked.

"I'll explain later," she said. "Now what can I do to help?"

I smiled and hugged her. "I've got a hunch about something, or maybe I should say, someone. Can you meet me in the parking lot at the bank around midnight?" Tori nodded in agreement. "We'll walk to the funeral home from there," I added.

"The funeral home?" Tori asked with surprise.

"The funeral home," I answered, "and, oh yes, please bring a camera."

CHAPTER 16

True to her word, Tori met me at the funeral home at midnight with camera in hand. "This place gives me the creeps," Tori muttered nervously as she held a flashlight and I picked the lock on the back door.

"I still don't see why we're here, though."

"Think about it," I replied. "Besides me, who had the most to gain from killing those people?"

"Maple?" Tori asked. "That's logical. He can't collect until after the funeral."

"Bingo," I said, as the lock clicked and I pushed the door open.

"I think they have a name for this," Tori said looking over her shoulder. "It's called breaking and entering."

"That's why I want you to stand outside and keep watch in case anybody comes," I said.

"All … all right," she said reluctantly. I crept into the room that served for deliveries and embalming.

As it had been the day I had visited Maple, the room was eerily illuminated by a single lamp. One embalming table had a body bag lying on it which looked like it was already occupied.

Suddenly I felt the presence of another person. I turned with a start. It was Tori. "I missed you," she said.

"Look, if you're having second thoughts …"

"No," she replied, as her grip cut off the blood supply to my arm.

"What is that awful smell?" Tori asked with disgust.

"Rotting flesh," I said with the best Dr. Thanatopsies imitation I could muster. Tori didn't appreciate my attempt at humor and pushed me along.

I unzipped the body bag and was shocked to find … Opal, and she looked like she'd been shrinkwrapped! I shone the light on the tag attached to the zipper. "What's it say?" I asked.

Tori struggled to read the tag in the darkness. "It says … her name is Jane Doe … and it looks like … she's being shipped to the dissection lab at Midwest Medical College!"

I walked over to a large wall with stainless steel drawers, took a deep breath and opened one. I pulled the sheet back on the body inside and shone the flashlight on the face. "Rachel McDowell?" I whispered to Tori. "But she was supposed to have been cremated! I went to the memorial service last week. Take a picture of her."

This just didn't make sense, I thought to myself. And then I had a hunch. I opened another drawer and pulled the sheet back. It was Esther Dale! With a great deal of coaxing, Tori came over and took another picture.

I opened a third drawer and found Gretta Von Heimlich. "That's it!" I exclaimed. "Maple is selling these bodies on the black market for medical research and this is how he preserves the bodies on ice until he's ready to ship them!"

"That's awful!" Tori snapped another picture.

All of a sudden, the electric garage door began to go up and both of us nearly jumped out of our skins.

"What are we gonna do now?" Tori asked.

I tried the only internal door that led into the funeral home, but it was locked from the other side. More and more light spilled into the room from a car's headlights as we panicked.

Tori pulled me over to Opal's body bag. "Get in!" she commanded.

"What?" I asked incredulously.

"There's no time to argue! Get in. They'll never find you in here."

"I'm not getting in there … with a naked corpse!"

"She's wrapped in plastic," Tori reminded me as she pushed from behind.

"But what about you? Where are you going to hide?" I asked.

"Don't worry about me," Tori replied. "Now get in, they're coming!"

With no other option, I climbed on to the table. "Move over Opal." Tori pushed me down in the bag. "Oooh … she's so cold and … stiff," I shuddered.

Tori pulled the zipper up to my chin. "I should have stayed in Hollywood."

I watched as Tori ran nearby to an empty open casket, climbed in, and pulled the lid partially shut. I managed to zip the body bag shut the rest of the way.

Maple Grove drove his long black hearse into the embalming room. Dr. Thanatopsies was riding shotgun. The two men got in the middle of what sounded like a very heated discussion. "I still don't see why we can't let one of my men do this run," complained Maple.

"It's getting too risky," the doctor replied. "Besides, I always enjoy visiting Midwest Medical College. Seeing my alma mater brings back such happy memories."

"Once we get rid of these bodies, I'm done," insisted Maple.

"Oh, no, you're not," growled Dr. Thanatopsies. "I just had a call today for another one."

"Well," Maple shrugged, "I just sold another pre-paid funeral package today. Some rich old dame named Cora. Easiest twenty grand I ever made."

Peeking from inside the casket, Tori gasped as the doctor attempted to lift the bottom of the bag that Opal and I were sharing. "How many bodies have you got in here?" he growled.

"Dead weight always carries heavy. Here, get underneath it, like this," Maple said, as he squatted down and got his shoulder underneath the top of the bag, pulling both Opal and me on to his back.

Dr. Thanatopsies attempted to follow Maple's instructions as he lifted the bottom of the bag.

Suddenly Maple set his end back down so it was only partially on the table. "Say, that reminds me, do you know what an Australian kiss is?"

Dr. Thanatopsies rolled his eyes as he gasped. "Help me …"

"It's the same thing as a French kiss," Maple continued, "except, down under! Get it? Down under."

Maple let loose with one of his hyena-like laughs which reverberated off the cold concrete walls. When he did, he let go of the bag and my head came crashing to the floor with a resounding thud.

"Shut up, you idiot!" Dr. Thanatopsies shouted. "They won't pay as much for damaged goods."

"You know, for a coroner, you don't have much of a sense of humor," Maple remarked as the two men picked the bag up again and threw Opal and me into the back of the hearse.

Unfortunately, Maple didn't realize the end with my head was still sticking out of the hearse about six inches. His slamming the door was the last thing I remember.

Sometime later, I'm not sure how long, I found myself waking up with a throbbing headache. It took me a few moments before I recalled what had happened and who I was with, or better put, who was underneath me. I managed to get my finger up to the top of the zipper so I could unzip it enough to see and get some air.

Dr. Thanatopsies was talking to an old man and a young woman. "Julie," the old man said, "this is Dr. Thanatopsies. He is one of our most distinguished graduates. He worked for me when he was a student here, too."

Dr. Thanatopsies extended his hand. "It's nice to meet you," he said, mustering as much charm as he was capable of, which still came out flat.

From my vantage point, the young woman appeared extremely shy, if not backward. "Nice to meet you," she replied without looking at him as she awkwardly shook his hand.

"I need to pay the good doctor, so he can be on his way. Would you please prepare the body?" the old man asked his young assistant.

"By myself?" she asked with panic in her voice.

"Yes, prepare it for tomorrow's dissection just as I showed you," the old man said reassuringly.

Prepare me for dissection! I had to get out of there.

"As I recall," the old man chuckled, "Dr. Thanatopsies was a little nervous his first day on the job, too."

The young woman wheeled me out as I heard the old man comment to Dr. Thanatopsies how unusual it was for so many indigent women to offer their bodies for medical research.

Julie wheeled Opal and me into another room. She locked the brakes and then left the room to answer a phone. Now was my chance!

I unzipped the bag, sat up and rubbed my head. "*What a nightmare!*" I muttered to myself.

I was just about to unzip the bag enough to get out when I heard Julie returning again. Lying back down in a panic, I zipped the bag shut again.

Julie walked over to the bag, took a deep breath, and gingerly unzipped it down as far as my chin. I kept my eyes straight ahead until she turned to pick up a scalpel from an instrument table, then I zipped the bag back up.

She turned back and looked at the bag in disbelief. After a moment, she laughed to herself to try and break the tension. Grasping the zipper firmly between her fingers, she unzipped it again.

When she turned back to pick up her scalpel again, I zipped the body bag back up again. "If somebody's playing a joke on me, I don't think it's funny!" Julie said, shaking as she surveyed the room.

For a third time, she unzipped the bag. This time with determination, I kept my eyes straight ahead, hoping she wouldn't notice the beads of perspiration breaking out on my face.

Now I know this whole thing sounds ridiculous, but I didn't know what else to do. Like everything else I had encountered, I had to make it up as I went along.

The young woman's hand was shaking as she brought the scalpel down to my face to make an incision—about six inches from my ear.

I knew I had run out of options. I reached up and grabbed her wrist. The poor girl screamed as she jumped back and flung the scalpel across the room.

To her horror, I sat up, unzipped the body bag the rest of the way, and stepped out. "Sorry, I already gave at the office," I muttered to her as I walked out leaving her frozen against a wall with her mouth hanging open.

I ran out of the dissection lab directly into the arms of Tori who was just rounding a corner, out of breath. "Sam! Thank goodness you're still in one piece!"

"Very funny! Where the hell have you been?"

"I never thought Maple was going to leave so I could get out of that casket!"

We ran out of the building and sped back toward Friendly in Tori's car to warn Cora and inform the authorities, certain we had discovered the true identity of the killers.

CHAPTER 17

It was about 10 a.m. when we drove by the charred sign posted at the city limits, and I saw the message left by the lightning:

WELCOME HOME

F IEND   !

The word "To," and the letters "*R*," "*L*," and "*Y*" had been knocked off.

"Look!" I exclaimed to Tori, as I slowed the car. "A special greeting, just for me!"

Tori laughed, "There's no place like home!"

"Ain't it the truth, ain't it the truth," I said in my best W. C. Fields incarnation. "Listen, after we check on Cora, I'm going to get the film developed."

"You're too late," Tori grinned. I dropped it off at the 24-hour photo lab on my way out of town."

"You mean I was stuck in that bag with Opal and you stopped to drop off film?"

Tori laughed as she nodded. "I figured you weren't going anywhere," she said, her eyes twinkling as they had that night on our first date. How could I possibly be mad at someone so beautiful. "And besides, I thought we might need the evidence."

"Good thinking," I said, as I laughed too and pulled into the parking lot of the town's only 24-hour photo lab.

The clerk appeared to be twenty-something, had purple hair, was covered with tattoos and had his body pierced every place that was visible, and probably in places that weren't. I wondered if he could be related to Willie at the nursing home. They appeared to be cut from the same cloth.

He had his feet up, his eyes closed, and was jerking to the beat of heavy metal that you could hear coming from the headphones on his head. Tori whispered to me, "He wasn't here when I dropped the film off."

We stood there a moment, hoping he would notice us. When he didn't, I reached over and turned off his Walkman. He looked up suddenly with a dull, sullen expression. "Hey, man!"

"I dropped off some film earlier," Tori said.

"What's the last name?" the clerk grunted.

"Epstein," Tori replied.

The clerk was fishing through all the envelopes until he came to one which had a note on it. "Oh, yeah," he said flatly, "the machine ate it."

I just about came across the counter at him. "The machine ate it!" I shouted.

The clerk jumped back. "Chill, dude! The company'll replace your film."

"The pictures on that film were irreplaceable!" I shouted. The clerk stepped back and studied me. His expression changed suddenly as the light dawned. "Hey," he said slowly. "Ain't you that dude who killed all those old ladies?"

Tori was looking through the envelopes. "Here it is!"

Talk about relief. I looked at Tori. It was time to leave.

"Dude, you're famous. I never met anybody famous." Then he leaned across the counter and asked in a hushed voice with an evil grin, "How'd you do it?"

I was at a loss for words.

Tori shot back, "He didn't do it! And I'll be back later to talk to the manager. Come on, Sam," Tori said, as she pulled me along after paying for the pictures. I left the store feeling it would probably be like this the rest of my life.

I held my breath as we opened the package in the car. The pictures were perfect. Every image was there: Rachel McDowell, Esther Dale, and especially Opal Thomas; all bagged and ready for shipping.

"I can't wait to see Neville's face when he sees these pictures of all my clients Maple said had been cremated."

"Whatever made you think to tell me to bring a camera?" Tori asked as we drove across town toward Buckeye Manor.

"Just a hunch," I shrugged.

"Pretty good one, if you ask me. Neville never would have thought of it." This girl sure seemed to know how to say all the right things.

We entered Buckeye Manor through the delivery entrance and made our way to Cora's room as quickly and quietly as possible.

We kept our eyes peeled for Nurse Swackhammer.

Tori knocked on the door and called to Cora. No answer. She knocked and called again. "She should be up by now," Tori said with concern in her voice as she pushed the door open and we crept in.

She wasn't in the living room, so Tori called again. "Aunt Cora." Tori's expression grew worried. We walked into the bedroom and froze in horror. Cora was lying on her bed, face up, with her eyes closed and her arms crossed. She was dressed in the clothes she had told me she wanted to be buried in!

"Oh no, we're too late!" Tori sobbed as she ran over and fell on her aunt. "I knew I should have come here instead of trying to rescue you. They've killed her and it's all my fault!"

Before I could respond, Cora opened her eyes and looked up.

"Land sakes, Child, you act as if somebody had died!"

"Aunt Cora," Tori cried, "You're alive! Thank God, you're alive!"

"Of course I'm alive. What ails you, Child?"

"She thought you had … well … that you …" I stammered.

"That I'd bitten the big one?" Cora said, as she composed herself and chuckled.

"Aunt Cora!" Tori exclaimed as I laughed to myself.

"I felt a little faint, so I just came in here to lie down."

"You felt a little faint?" Tori lamented with her best Jewish mother incarnation. "I'll go get you a glass of water."

"Really Child, I'm fine," Cora said reassuringly. "But if it will make you feel better, there's a glass by the sink in the bathroom," she added. Tori went into Cora's bathroom to get her a drink of water.

"I'm always glad to see you, Sam, but if they catch you here …"

"I know," I said standing over her, "but we came to warn you …"

Just then there was a knock on Cora's bedroom door. I turned around and it was Nurse Swackhammer who had walked in carrying a tray of medication.

When she saw me standing over Cora, she screamed, and flung the tray with all its contents at me. "He's done it again! Murderer! Murderer!"

I followed her from Cora's bedroom into the living room to try and explain, but she started screaming again and ran out of the apartment shouting she was going to call the Sheriff.

I stood there by the door wondering if I should follow her, when Cora's refrigerator started one of its epileptic fits, except this time it was worse than anything I had ever heard before. It shook ... it banged ... it shuddered, until finally it gave out a horrible groan and died, whereupon the refrigerator door swung open slowly with a creak in one last desperate attempt to purge itself of the deep dark secret hidden within.

I cocked my head and looked at the contents with a puzzled expression which slowly changed to disbelief. I wasn't surprised that it was practically empty. Most residents took their meals in the common dining room since it was included in the monthly fee.

"Stop!" Cora cried as she emerged from her bedroom with Tori. "You'll let that man out of ..." But it was too late.

Tori walked up beside me, looked at the contents and then at me with the same puzzled expression as mine. We couldn't believe our eyes: a plate with slices of fruitcake, a pair of yellow rubber gloves, and a bedpan full of white powder.

We both turned toward Cora who looked like the cat that swallowed the canary. "the refrigerator ..." Cora said, sounding deflated.

"Cora, what is the meaning of this?" I demanded.

The sound of sirens filled the air as Sheriff Weems and his deputy roared up the drive.

"I'm sorry, Sam," Cora said. "I know I've been a bad girl, but those old ladies weren't happy."

"So you murdered them? Aunt Cora, how could you?" Tori cried in disbelief while Cora bit her lip and stared at the floor. She looked like a five-year-old child reacting to a scolding after getting caught with her hand in the cookie jar.

"What about Mr. Nofzinger?" I asked. Cora looked up at me. "I never intended to hurt you, Sam, and I knew he wasn't one of your clients, so I hoped it might throw them off the track. Besides, he said some things about you I didn't like."

Suddenly, Sheriff Weems burst in with gun drawn, accompanied by Detective Foltze and Nurse Swackhammer. "But I thought you said she was dead!" Sheriff Weems shouted as he turned toward the nurse.

"Well," Nurse Swackhammer stammered, "she was, or at least, I thought she was." By now, Muffie had arrived, carrying the preserved remains of her beloved Rush.

Cora looked around at everyone and with a sense of the dramatic, and said, "Sheriff, I want to confess."

"Confess to what?" Neville bellowed as he burst through the door. Good old Nurse Swackhammer had called him as well. Neville glared at Tori who had her arm around mine.

"Miss Merriweather," the Sheriff replied gravely, "ever since I had the privilege of sitting under your instruction in high school, I have had nothing but the highest respect for you. But you must realize, this is not a game. A man's life is at stake here."

Cora looked over at me with eyes which begged for forgiveness. "I am so sorry, Sam. It is all my fault that all this has happened to you. I killed those old people … every last one of them."

"How did you know which ones were my clients?" I asked. "I never told you."

"No," Cora replied, "you didn't. But Nurse Swackhammer can be a wealth of information." All of us turned toward Nurse Swackhammer who looked like she was going to fall right through the floor.

"You are saying you killed all five of them?" Neville asked Cora skeptically.

"Five? Oh, they weren't the first."

"You mean there were others?" Muffie gasped as she turned white.

The edges of Cora's mouth turned up slightly with just the hint of a sadistic little smile. "They were just the first ones anyone ever noticed."

Neville jumped in. "Sam Majors, this is just another one of your ruses to cover your tracks. And it's pretty pathetic, attempting to get this dear old lady whom we all love and respect to …"

Cora looked up with fire in her eyes as she cut him off in mid-sentence. "Neville Longworth, for once in your life, shut up!

You are still as dull and unimaginative as you were when I had you as a student." Neville shrank back as Tori and I tried to keep from snickering.

"You are a large part of the reason I did it to those last four women, Neville," Cora continued. "If Sam Majors had some incentive to stay, maybe, I thought, my beautiful niece might avoid being saddled with you for the rest of her life. Don't think I don't have eyes. I know what you were up to. The only thing you didn't count on, that many of you didn't count on, was Sam Majors coming back to Friendly to take over his mother's practice, let alone making a go of it. I just thought I'd help him along a bit, and maybe, after he'd been able to put a little money aside, he could go back out West and take Tori with him. There's no future for her here."

I looked at Cora in disbelief.

"I didn't want you to lose your dream, Sam, like I lost mine. Besides, those old people weren't happy, not really. Everything they loved in life had been taken away from them. Oh, I know all of you think it was wrong of me to play God, and maybe you're right. But do any of you really know how it feels to sit, day after day, staring at the walls, hoping and praying that someone, anyone, will come and visit you, to let you know they care, while you just sit there and wait to check out? I do. It's enough to make you crazy. So, I decided to give them "A Little Taste of Heaven" —just a little ahead of schedule. Think they'd come back if they had the chance? I doubt it."

"Miss Merriweather," Sheriff Weems interrupted.

"I know, I know," Cora cut him off with a wave of her hand, "I have the right to remain silent ..." Cora steeled her face as she dramatically stuck out her hands to be cuffed.

"That won't be necessary," he said.

Deputy Foltze interrupted. "Sheriff, we'd better get her out of here. The press knows something is up. The downstairs lobby is swarming with cameramen. *Neville had been at it again,* I thought to myself. *Great publicity for his next election campaign.*

"Cameras? May I have just a moment to fix my makeup?" Cora asked.

The deputy shook his head "no" at the Sheriff who ignored him. "Sure, Miss Merriweather," Sheriff Weems said.

"Would you like me to help, Aunt Cora?" Tori asked.

"No, child, I can do it myself," Cora replied.

"Only a moment," Sheriff Weems cautioned her.

After Cora left to go to her bedroom, there was an awkward silence until Tori shouted, "Sheriff!" We all jumped about three feet. "I almost forgot. Mr. Majors has something to show you!" She pulled the pictures out of her purse and thrust them into my hand.

She then began to explain, "In the process of trying to clear his good name, Sam Majors has uncovered a criminal conspiracy to sell the bodies of Buckeye Manor residents on the black market for medical research after they were supposed to have been cremated."

I thought Nurse Swackhammer's eyes were going to pop out of their sockets. Muffie was so shaken that she dropped Rush on his head, which broke off and rolled across the floor, cigarette lighter and all.

Tori continued, "I demand that the County Prosecutor dismiss the charges against Mr. Majors, and charge Dr. Thanatopsies and Maple Grove!" In less than 10 minutes, I had gone from victim to victor.

The Sheriff handed the pictures to Neville who couldn't believe his eyes. "Well, Mr. Prosecutor?"

Neville handed the pictures back to the Sheriff and threw his hands up in exasperation. "I give up!" he shouted as he stalked off in a huff. After collecting the pieces of her beloved Rush, Muffie and Nurse Swackhammer weren't far behind, leaving I presumed, to inform their cohorts of our discovery.

"Come election time, looks to me like we may be needing a new prosecutor," Sheriff Weems said with a grin.

"Good," Tori grinned as she looked at me. "I know just the man for the job! If he wants it," she added.

Several cameramen appeared at the door to Cora's apartment.

The Sheriff was growing impatient. "What's keeping her?"

I followed the Sheriff and Tori into Cora's bedroom where we found her seated in front of her makeup table staring into the mirror, now wearing her red sequin dress. Sitting on the table next to her was a framed glamour shot of herself like the one she'd had sitting on her piano.

It was evident, to me at least, that she was trying to make herself look like she had in that picture so many years before.

All of a sudden I saw Cora Merriweather in a totally different light and it made me sad. Despite all she had put me through, I felt sorry for her. She was a tragic figure—pathetic, really. All those years living her life to accommodate the desires of others, repressing her dreams and her true sense of self, had forced her to create her own little fantasy world. Mom's words in the hospital came back to me, "To thine own self be true, then thou canst not then be false to any man."

I decided then and there I wasn't going to suffer Cora's fate of feeling trapped by my circumstances, and I had a feeling that Tori was going to play a part in helping me realize my dreams.

"Aunt Cora," Tori said gently, "we'd better go. More and more cameras are arriving."

Cora sat up very imperiously with the same distant look in her eyes I'd seen that day in her apartment when she'd quoted Norma Desmond's dialogue in *Sunset Boulevard*. She had slipped into the persona of the famous movie star once again.

"They have? Tell them I'll be on the set at once."

I did not realize the significance of it at the time, but Cora slipped something into her mouth that she'd been holding in her hand. I presumed it to be her blood pressure medication.

"Hey, what is this?" the Sheriff asked skeptically.

I took him aside. "I've seen this before, Sheriff. She thinks this is *Sunset Boulevard* and she's Gloria Swanson."

"What? This better not be some kind of gimmick to cop an insanity plea."

"It's no gimmick. Believe me. It's the easiest way to get her downstairs."

Cora emerged at the top of the grand staircase in the Buckeye Manor lobby with Tori and me supporting her on either side and Sheriff Weems close behind.

Letting Tori hold Cora's arm, I bounded down the stairs as the media surged forward shouting "What's happening up there?" "Any statement?" "Is it true she confessed?" "Why did she do it?"

"Are you ready, Cora?" I shouted up to her, hoping to keep the fantasy going long enough to coax her downstairs.

Cora squinted as she looked into the glare of the camera lights and sea of reporters. "What is the scene? Where am I?"

"This is Columbia Pictures!" I improvised.

"Oh, yes. Down below. They're waiting for my close-up!"

"All right," I shouted. "Ready! Cameras! Action!"

As Cora descended the grand staircase for her last great entrance, I couldn't help but be reminded of William Holden's narrative in the last scene of the movie that Cora was finally getting to live out.

"So they were turning after all. Those cameras. Life which can be strangely merciful had taken pity on Norma Desmond. The dream she had clung to so desperately had enfolded her."

Several steps from the bottom, Cora stopped. Like Gloria Swanson in the climactic scene from *Sunset Boulevard*, Cora waved her hand over her head as she quoted the dialogue from the movie letter perfect.

"I can't go on with the scene. I'm too happy. I just want you to know how glad I am to be back in the studio making a picture. You don't know how I've missed this, and I promise I'll never desert you again. We'll make another picture and another and another.

You see, this is my life and it always will be. There's nothing else. Just us and the cameras. And those wonderful people out there in the dark. All right, I'm ready for my close-up."

At that point, Cora collapsed on the stairs. When she fell, she landed with her arm extended and her palm up. In her outstretched hand was her handkerchief which contained the remnants of a partially eaten piece of fruitcake.

"Quick. Call an ambulance!" the Sheriff shouted.

But it was too late. Cora was pronounced dead on arrival at the hospital. An autopsy revealed she had eaten fruitcake laced with the same poison she had used on all the others. She must have slipped it into her mouth while she was at her make-up table, knowing death would follow shortly thereafter.

A case of "just desserts" if ever there was one.

Things seemed to move pretty quickly from then on. As much as he hated to do it, Neville was forced to dismiss the charges against me, while Maple Grove and Dr. Thanatopsies became the ones put on ice in state prison, thanks to the generosity of the good people of the State of Ohio.

And, with the help of Judge Corbin, Pauline got her house back, after it turned out Jane O'Donnel had prepared the deed herself, using the wrong legal description. Aaron Longworth never had anything to do with it after all!

As for the heir apparent, Neville decided to take a long, long vacation.

With the threat of closure by the state licensing authorities, Muffie agreed to sell Buckeye Manor to a reputable company that operated several other nursing homes in the State.

Given the notoriety that her brother's fruitcake received, Muffie and Waldo Pride decided to market his confection across the country under a new name: "A Taste To Die For."

Dad eventually came home determined to resume his practice of law, which would create new problems for me to solve as his body began to outlive his mind.

When things had finally quieted down a bit, Tori and I went back to clean out Cora's apartment. As we were leaving, Audrey ran up and grabbed me by the arm. With tears in her eyes she said, "You remember that day in the chapel? Well, you were right, confession is good for the soul. I was crying because I had told my boyfriend I hated him and that I never wanted to see him again. But I took your advice and told him the truth about the baby coming, and see …" Grinning from ear to ear, she held up her ring finger to show me a tiny solitaire diamond. "We're going to be married!"

"Congratulations, Audrey," I said warmly. "I'm so happy for you."

As we turned to leave, Audrey grabbed Tori's arm and whispered, "Your Aunt Cora was right when she told me that it's better to pick a barrel of apples that'll keep through the winter."

Tori smiled. "I know, Audrey, oh how I know."

As for Tori and me, well … the fairy tale continues.

Did my dreams of becoming a writer ever come true?

Well, here I am … and there you are reading this, and well … maybe Dad was right after all. Sometimes a detour is the most direct path on life's great adventure.

The End

www.ingramcontent.com/pod-product-compliance
Lightning Source LLC
Chambersburg PA
CBHW020607250626
47154CB00004B/1399